READ & LISTEN OS MELHORES CONTOS DO SÉCULO XX EM VERSÃO ORIGINAL NA ÍNTEGRA

"Sometimes all we need is a fine, short story."

Martins Fontes

James Baldwin
Sonny's Blues

•

Jack London
A Piece of Steak

© 1957 por James Baldwin. Esta edição foi publicada em acordo com James Baldwin Estate.
© 2011 Martins Editora Livraria Ltda.,
São Paulo, para a presente edição.

Publisher	*Evandro Mendonça Martins Fontes*
Coordenação editorial	*Anna Dantes*
Produção editorial	*Alyne Azuma*
Tradução	*Ana Luiza Couto*
Preparação	*Magda França Lopes*
Revisão	*Denise Roberti Camargo*
	Mariana Zanini
	Dinarte Zorzanelli da Silva
Biografias e apresentações	*Laura Fernández*
Locução de "Sonny's Blues"	*Juba Zaki*
Locução de "A Piece of Steak"	*David Tamke*
Gravação	*RecLab*
Técnico	*Francesc Gosalves*

Dados Internacionais de Catalogação na Publicação (CIP)
(Câmara Brasileira do Livro, SP, Brasil)

Baldwin, James, 1924-1987.
   Sonny's Blues / James Baldwin. A piece of steak / Jack London / ; [tradução Ana Luiza Couto]. -- São Paulo : Martins Martins Fontes, 2011.

   Título original: Sonny's blues ; A piece of steak
   Inclui CD.
   ISBN 978-85-863-004-6

   1. Ficção norte-americana I. London, Jack, 1876-1916. II. Título. III. Título: A piece of steak.

11-01803   CDD-813

Índices para catálogo sistemático:
1. Ficção : Literatura norte-americana   813

Todos os direitos desta edição para o Brasil reservados à
Martins Editora Livraria Ltda.
Av. Dr. Arnaldo, 2076
01255-000 São Paulo SP Brasil
Tel. (11) 3116.0000
info@martinseditora.com.br
www.martinsmartinsfontes.com.br

SUMÁRIO

INTRODUÇÃO 9

James Baldwin
BIOGRAFIA. 13
APRESENTAÇÃO DO CONTO 15
Sonny's Blues 17

Jack London
BIOGRAFIA 73
APRESENTAÇÃO DO CONTO 75
A Piece of Steak 77

INTRODUÇÃO
Dê um passo além e leia os clássicos em versão original

Para muitos de nós, ler em versão original supõe um desafio por vezes irrealizável. Habituados a nossa própria língua, ficamos frustrados quando não entendemos todas as palavras de um texto. Quantas vezes deixamos um livro de lado porque não queremos consultar o dicionário a toda hora? Essa consulta (quase sempre obrigatória) se soma ao desconhecimento das referências culturais, à dificuldade de perceber os matizes, a ironia do autor etc. Logo nos aborrecemos por não conseguir compreender a essência do relato e acabamos fechando o livro e buscando a versão traduzida.

Na coleção READ & LISTEN a leitura e audição do texto original produzem experiências tão únicas quanto a de contemplar uma pintura em vez de sua reprodução. Não só se aprende como também se desfruta e assimila o verdadeiro espírito do relato.

Aqui, os leitores podem ter acesso aos melhores contos dos mais respeitados autores de língua inglesa, com as ferramentas necessárias para compreender os textos em sua totalidade.

Foi-se o tempo de ler com o dicionário do lado. Cada conto inclui um extenso glossário para que não seja necessário interromper a leitura. Além de todas as palavras que você pode não entender, ele apresenta referências culturais, deixa claras as nuances e permite compreender todos os toques irônicos de cada conto. Para quem quer praticar a compreensão oral ou simplesmente ouvir o texto enquanto o lê, nada mais simples. Ponha o CD com a versão em áudio dos contos para tocar, sente-se, relaxe e deixe que um locutor nativo conte a história. Porque não há maneira melhor de colocar ao seu alcance essas obras-primas do que rompendo as barreiras que o mantiveram longe delas durante tanto tempo.

Quem tem medo dos clássicos?

E por falar em clássicos... Nossa seleção se guiou por várias premissas: em primeiro lugar, os contos tinham de ser sugestivos e não muito complexos; em segundo lugar, tinham de representar o mundo próprio de cada autor. Clássicos em miniatura, inesquecíveis, os contos desta coleção devem ser lidos com cuidado, degustando cada frase, cada palavra. São obras capazes de transformar seus personagens em alguém conhecido, quase familiar, que poderia ser seu melhor amigo.

Acreditamos que, depois de tanto tempo aprendendo inglês, chegou seu momento de desfrutar. Você merece.

James Baldwin
Sonny's Blues

"He hit something in all of them, he hit something in me, myself, and the music tightened and deepened, apprehension began to beat the air. Creole began to tell us what the blues were all about."

BIOGRAFIA
James Baldwin

Aos 14 anos queria ser pregador. Muitos anos depois, em 1953, converteu aquele desvio religioso numa obra-prima chamada *Vá dizê-lo na montanha*. James Baldwin (Nova York, 1924 – Saint-Paul-de-Vence, França, 1987) era o mais velho de nove irmãos, e o assunto de pregador veio à baila porque, na verdade, seu pai exercia essa função no Harlem, bairro onde cresceu sua enorme família – também retratada com maestria incomparável nesse primeiro romance, no qual Baldwin talhou um personagem à sua semelhança, o de John Grimes.

Cansado de seu bairro, de sua família e da asfixiante atmosfera racista dos Estados Unidos nos anos 1940, muito antes de publicar seu primeiro romance e antes que o mundo soubesse que o pequeno James seria um grande escritor, mudou-se para a França (Paris foi seu segundo lar). Na França escreveu *The Amen Corner* (1954), uma obra de teatro crítica em relação aos fiéis da igreja negra que tinha suas raízes novamente naquela precoce experiência religiosa. Ainda que tenha sido concluído em 1955, *The Amen Corner* [O canto do amém] não foi publicado até 1968. Antes chegariam às livrarias sua coleção de ensaios *Notes of a Native Son* [Notas de um filho nativo] (1955), cinco romances e uma antologia de contos, *Going to Meet the Man* [Indo encontrar o homem] (1965), na qual está incluído o fantástico conto "Sonny's Blues".

Giovanni, de 1956, é o puro romance de protesto, em que o autor fala pela primeira vez da homossexualidade. Um ano depois de seu lançamento, o escritor regressou aos Estados Unidos, onde publicou, em 1961, outra coleção de ensaios combativos, *Nobody Knows My Name* [Ninguém sabe meu nome], à qual se seguiram os romances *Another Country* [Outro país], em 1962, e *The Fire Next Time*, em 1963, duas histórias que tratam do conflito racial. Um ano depois, publicou sua segunda peça de teatro, *Blues for Mister Charlie* [Blues para o senhor Charlie], uma crônica brutal sobre o linchamento de um jovem negro, seguida, em 1968, pela frustrada história de amor entre um ator negro e uma atriz branca em *Tell me How Long the Train's Been Gone* [Diga-me há quanto tempo o trem partiu].

No final dos anos 1960, especialmente depois do assassinato de Martin Luther King em 1968, Baldwin juntou-se ao *Black Power* – movimento negro de luta pela cidadania. Sua influência pode ser notada nos ensaios *No Name in the Street* [Sem nome na rua] (1972) e *The Devil Finds Work* [O diabo encontra trabalho] (1976), mas sobretudo no célebre romance *If Beale Street Could Talk* [Se a rua Beale pudesse falar], de 1974, sobre um jovem negro preso injustamente. Seu último romance mais famoso foi *Just Above My Head* [Logo acima da cabeça], que narra a história de um grupo de amigos dados a cantar nas igrejas do Harlem, publicado em 1979.

James, que o poeta Richard Wright disse ser "o melhor escritor negro do mundo", foi amigo íntimo de Nina Simone, e habitualmente a presenteava com livros que acabaram influenciando as canções dela. Mas se alguém o apontou como influência direta foi a Prêmio Nobel Toni Morrison, que considerava sua a luta de Baldwin. A obra de Baldwin, romancista da face menos amável dos EUA pós-guerra, poderia resumir-se numa frase extraída de um dos contos de *Going to Meet the Man*: "Não sofrer é impossível, mas lutamos para encontrar a maneira de evitar afogar-nos no sofrimento".

LAURA FERNÁNDEZ

APRESENTAÇÃO DO CONTO
Sonny's Blues

Esta é a história de dois irmãos que nunca se compreenderam totalmente. Dois irmãos que partilharam brinquedos, pais, momentos ruins, e que acabaram impelidos a dois extremos da vida. Um se fez professor – consciente de que a única coisa que um garoto negro de família pobre podia fazer para sair do Harlem era estudar. O outro resolveu tocar piano e acabou desaparecendo numa espiral de destruição que levou seu nome às manchetes (não exatamente positivas). A heroína esteve a ponto de mandá-lo para o outro lado. Mas não o fez. E agora o bom garoto precisa entender por que a música é tudo para seu irmão Sonny.

Publicado originalmente na antologia *Going to Meet the Man*, "Sonny's Blues" é, sem dúvida, um dos melhores contos de James Baldwin, autor que sempre esteve ao lado do oprimido (sua luta literária em favor da comunidade negra e dos homossexuais sempre foi implacável) e que, nesta ocasião, desembainha todas as suas armas: um diálogo incisivo, uma descrição do ambiente brutal e uma relação, a dos dois irmãos, absolutamente realista.

Como se instalasse uma câmera na sala do protagonista, o conto se sucede como um tipo de documentário sobre a relação entre os dois irmãos ao longo do tempo. A condição de garotos pobres do Harlem os acompanha durante o fragmento de vida narrado e sustenta toda a trama, apoiada muito claramente na paixão que Sonny sente pelo jazz, única mão que, depois de tudo, consegue tirá-lo do buraco.

Para uma completa compreensão do texto se pode recorrer aos glossários que aparecem em cada página. O vocabulário que encontraremos está relacionado com a música, com os carros (por meio de um cruel episódio do passado), com o ensino (já que o protagonista é professor) e, claro, com a vida familiar, em toda a sua extensão. Em qualquer caso, "Sonny's Blues" não é um texto extremamente complexo; uma das constantes da obra de Baldwin e um dos motivos principais de seu êxito foi sua prosa fluida e transparente, que contrasta por completo com a áspera e enigmática realidade descrita.

Com os anos 1950 como pano de fundo (e uma cruel história de racismo no seio de sua família, da qual a mãe não se atreve a falar até que seja tarde demais), "Sonny's Blues" mergulha o leitor na periferia de Nova York, algo que Baldwin conhecia bem. O próprio autor cresceu no Harlem, e esta história parece ter saído das entranhas dele. Parece que estamos ouvindo sua voz (e a versão em áudio do conto, incluída nesta edição, permite uma compreensão e um mergulho ainda maiores), a voz do garoto que cresceu acreditando que tudo estava perdido e que, graças à literatura, conseguiu escapar de seu destino. Os irmãos também funcionam assim, como uma espécie de *alter ego* do escritor, sempre tratando de capturar o infortúnio do condenado.

LAURA FERNÁNDEZ

Sonny's Blues

I READ ABOUT IT in the paper, in the subway[1], on my way to work. I read it, and I couldn't believe it, and I read it again. Then perhaps I just stared at it, at the newsprint[2] spelling out[3] his name, spelling out the story. I stared at it in the swinging lights of the subway car[4], and in the faces and bodies of the people, and in my own face, trapped in the darkness which roared outside.

It was not to be believed and I kept telling myself that, as I walked from the subway station to the high school. And at the same time I couldn't doubt it. I was scared, scared for Sonny. He became real to me again. A great block of ice got settled in my belly[5] and kept melting[6] there slowly all day long, while I taught my classes algebra. It was a special kind of ice. It kept melting, sending trickles[7] of ice water all up and down my veins, but it never got less. Sometimes it hardened[8] and seemed to expand until I felt my guts were going to come spilling out[9] or that I was going to choke[10] or scream. This would always be at a moment when I was remembering some specific thing Sonny had once said or done.

When he was about as old as the boys in my classes his

---

1 **subway:** metrô • 2 **newsprint:** jornal • 3 **spelling out:** soletrando • 4 **the swinging lights of the subway car:** as luzes flutuantes do vagão do metrô • 5 **got settled in my belly:** se instalou em minha barriga • 6 **kept melting:** foi se derretendo • 7 **trickles:** gotas • 8 **it hardened:** endureceu • 9 **I felt my guts were going to come spilling out:** sentia que ia botar os bofes pela boca • 10 **choke:** asfixiar

face had been bright and open, there was a lot of copper[1] in it; and he'd had wonderfully direct brown eyes, and great gentleness[2] and privacy. I wondered what he looked like now. He had been picked up[3], the evening before, in a raid[4] on an apartment downtown, for peddling[5] and using heroin.

I couldn't believe it: but what I mean by that is that I couldn't find any room[6] for it anywhere inside me. I had kept it outside me for a long time. I hadn't wanted to know. I had had suspicions, but I didn't name them, I kept putting them away[7]. I told myself that Sonny was wild, but he wasn't crazy. And he'd always been a good boy, he hadn't ever turned hard[8] or evil or disrespectful, the way kids can, so quick, so quick, especially in Harlem. I didn't want to believe that I'd ever see my brother going down, coming to nothing, all that light in his face gone out, in the condition I'd already seen so many others. Yet it had happened and here I was, talking about algebra to a lot of boys who might, every one of them for all I knew, be popping off needles[9] every time they went to the head[10]. Maybe it did more for them than algebra could.

I was sure that the first time Sonny had ever had horse, he couldn't have been much older than these boys were now. These boys, now, were living as we'd been living then, they were growing up with a rush[11] and their heads bumped[12] abruptly against the low ceiling of their actual possibilities. They were filled with rage. All they really knew were two

---

1 **copper:** cor de cobre • 2 **gentleness:** doçura • 3 **he had been picked up:** havia sido detido • 4 **raid:** batida policial • 5 **peddling:** traficar • 6 **room:** espaço • 7 **I kept putting them away:** seguia postergando-os • 8 **hard:** insensível • 9 **popping off needles:** chutando • 10 **head:** mente • 11 **with a rush:** a toda velocidade • 12 **bumped:** chocavam

darknesses, the darkness of their lives, which was now closing in on them[1], and the darkness of the movies, which had blinded them[2] to that other darkness, and in which they now, vindictively[3], dreamed, at once more together than they were at any other time, and more alone.

When the last bell rang, the last class ended, I let out my breath. It seemed I'd been holding it[4] for all that time. My clothes were wet—I may have looked as though I'd been sitting in a steam bath[5], all dressed up, all afternoon. I sat alone in the classroom a long time. I listened to the boys outside, downstairs, shouting and cursing[6] and laughing. Their laughter struck me[7] for perhaps the first time. It was not the joyous laughter which—God knows why—one associates with children. It was mocking and insular[8], its intent was to denigrate. It was disenchanted, and in this, also, lay the authority of them curses. Perhaps I was listening to them because I was thinking about my brother and in them I heard my brother. And myself.

One boy was whistling a tune, at once very complicated and very simple, it seemed to be pouring out of him[9] as though he were a bird, and it sounded very cool and moving through all that harsh[10], bright air, only just holding its own through all those other sounds.

I stood up and walked over to the window and looked down into the courtyard. It was the beginning of the spring

---

1 **was now closing in on them:** estava agora se fechando sobre eles • 2 **had blinded them:** os havia impedido de ver • 3 **vindictively:** com desejo de vingança • 4 **holding it:** segurando-o • 5 **steam bath:** banho turco; sauna a vapor • 6 **cursing:** xingando • 7 **their laughter struck me:** suas risadas me chamaram a atenção • 8 **mocking and insular:** zombeteira e isolada • 9 **pouring out of him:** sair dele • 10 **harsh:** violento

and the sap¹ was rising in the boys. A teacher passed through them every now and again, quickly, as though he or she couldn't wait to get out of that courtyard², to get those boys out of their sight and off their minds. I started collecting my stuff. I thought I'd better get home and talk to Isabel.

The courtyard was almost deserted by the time I got downstairs. I saw this boy standing in the shadow of a doorway, looking just like Sonny. I almost called his name. Then I saw that it wasn't Sonny, but somebody we used to know, a boy from around our block. He'd been Sonny's friend. He'd never been mine, having been too young for me, and, anyway, I'd never liked him. And now, even though he was a grown-up³ man, he still hung around⁴ that block, still spent hours on the street corners, was always high and raggy⁵. I used to run into him⁶ from time to time and he'd often work around to asking me for⁷ a quarter or fifty cents. He always had some real good excuse, too, and I always gave it to him, I don't know why.

But now, abruptly, I hated him. I couldn't stand⁸ the way he looked at me, partly like a dog, partly like a cunning⁹ child. I wanted to ask him what the hell he was doing in the school courtyard.

He sort of shuffled over to me¹⁰, and he said, "I see you got the papers. So you already know about it."

"You mean about Sonny? Yes, I already know about it.

---

1 **sap:** seiva (aqui, metaforicamente, "sangue") • 2 **courtyard:** pátio • 3 **grown-up:** adulto • 4 **hung around:** rondava • 5 **high and raggy:** alto e esfarrapado • 6 **run into him:** encontrar com ele • 7 **work around to asking me for:** resolvia me pedir • 8 **I couldn't stand:** não suportava • 9 **cunning:** astuto • 10 **he sort of shuffled over to me:** meio que se aproximou arrastando os pés

How come[1] they didn't get you?"

He grinned. It made him repulsive and it also brought to mind what he'd looked like as a kid. "I wasn't there. I stay away from them people."

"Good for you." I offered him a cigarette and I watched him through the smoke. "You come all the way down here just to tell me about Sonny?"

"That's right." He was sort of shaking his head and his eyes looked strange, as though they were about to cross. The bright sun deadened[2] his damp[3] dark brown skin and it made his eyes look yellow and showed up the dirt in his kinked[4] hair. He smelled funky[5]. I moved a little away from him and I said, "Well, thanks. But I already know about it and I got to get home."

"I'll walk you a little ways," he said. We started walking. There were a couple of kids still loitering[6] in the courtyard and one of them said goodnight to me and looked strangely at the boy beside me.

"What're you going to do?" he asked me. "I mean, about Sonny?"

"Look. I haven't seen Sonny for over a year, I'm not sure I'm going to do anything. Anyway, what the hell *can* I do?"

"That's right," he said quickly, "ain't nothing you can do[7]. Can't much help old Sonny no more, I guess."

It was what I was thinking and so it seemed to me he had no right to say it.

---

1 **how come…?:** como é que…? • 2 **deadened:** atenuava • 3 **damp:** úmida • 4 **kinked :** enrolado • 5 **he smelled funky:** fedia • 6 **loitering:** vadiando • 7 **ain't nothing (there's nothing) you can do:** não pode fazer nada

"I'm surprised at Sonny, though," he went on—he had a funny way of talking, he looked straight ahead as though he were talking to himself—"I thought Sonny was a smart boy, I thought he was too smart to get hung[1]."

"I guess he thought so too," I said sharply, "and that's how he got hung. And now about you? You're pretty goddamn smart[2], I bet."

Then he looked directly at me, just for a minute. "I ain't smart[3]," he said. "If I was smart, I'd have reached for a pistol a long time ago."

"Look. Don't tell *me* your sad story, if it was up to me[4], I'd give you one." Then I felt guilty—guilty, probably, for never having supposed that the poor bastard *had* a story of his own, much less a sad one, and I asked, quickly, "What's going to happen to him now?"

He didn't answer this. He was off by himself[5] some place. "Funny thing[6]," he said, and from his tone we might have been discussing the quickest way to get to Brooklyn, "when I saw the papers this morning, the first thing I asked myself was if I had anything to do with it[7]. I felt sort of responsible."

I began to listen more carefully. The subway station was on the corner, just before us, and I stopped. He stopped, too. We were in front of a bar and he ducked slightly[8], peering in[9], but whoever he was looking for didn't seem to be there. The juke box was blasting away[10] with something black and bouncy[11]

---

1 **get hung:** se deixou pegar • 2 **goddamn smart:** desgraçadamente esperto • 3 **I ain't smart (I'm not smart):** não sou esperto • 4 **if it was up to me:** se dependesse de mim • 5 **he was off by himself:** havia se isolado • 6 **funny thing:** é engraçado • 7 **if I had anything to do with it:** se eu tinha alguma coisa a ver com isso • 8 **he ducked slightly:** se agachou um pouco • 9 **peering in:** olhou para dentro • 10 **the juke box was blasting away:** a *jukebox* estava a todo volume • 11 **bouncy:** alegre, animado

and I half watched the barmaid as she danced her way from the juke box to her place behind the bar. And I watched her face as she laughingly responded to something someone said to her, still keeping time to the music. When she smiled one saw the little girl, one sensed the doomed[1], still-struggling woman beneath the battered[2] face of the semi-whore[3].

"I never *give* Sonny nothing," the boy said finally, "but a long time ago I come to school high and Sonny asked me how it felt." He paused, I couldn't bear[4] to watch him, I watched the barmaid, and I listened to the music which seemed to be causing the pavement to shake[5]. "I told him it felt great." The music stopped, the barmaid paused and watched the juke box until the music began again. "It did."

All this was carrying me some place I didn't want to go. I certainly didn't want to know how it felt. It filled everything, the people, the houses, the music, the dark, quicksilver[6] barmaid, with menace[7]; and this menace was their reality.

"What's going to happen to him now?" I asked again.

They'll send him away some place and they'll try to cure him." He shook his head[8]. "Maybe he'll even think he's kicked the habit[9]. Then they'll let him loose[10]"—he gestured, throwing his cigarette into the gutter[11]. "That's all."

"What do you mean, that's *all*?"

But I knew what he meant.

"I *mean*, that's *all*." He turned his head and looked at me,

---

1 **doomed:** condenada • 2 **battered:** maltratada • 3 **whore:** puta • 4 **I couldn't bear:** não podia suportar • 5 **causing the pavement to shake:** fazendo o solo tremer • 6 **quicksilver:** volúvel • 7 **menace:** ameaça • 8 **he shook his head:** negou com a cabeça • 9 **he's kicked the habit:** largar o vício •10 **they'll let him loose:** o soltarão • 11 **gutter:** sarjeta

pulling down the corners of his mouth[1]. "Don't you know what I mean?" he asked, softly.

"How the hell *would* I know what you mean?" I almost whispered it, I don't know why.

That's right," he said to the air, "how would *he* know what I mean?" He turned toward me again, patient and calm, and yet I somehow felt him shaking, shaking as though he were going to fall apart. I felt that ice in my guts again, the dread[2] I'd felt all afternoon; and again I watched the barmaid, moving about the bar, washing glasses, and singing. "Listen. They'll let him out and then it'll just start all over again. That's what I mean."

"You mean—they'll let him out. And then he'll just start working his way back in again. You mean hell never kick the habit. Is that what you mean?"

"That's right," he said, cheerfully[3]. "*You* see what I mean."

"Tell me," I said it last, "why does he want to die? He must want to die, he's killing himself, why does he want to die?"

He looked at me in surprise. He licked his lips. "He don't want to die. He wants to live. Don't nobody want to die, ever."

Then I wanted to ask him—too many things. He could not have answered, or if he had, I could not have borne the answers. I started walking. "Well, I guess it's none of my business[4]."

"It's going to be rough[5] on old Sonny," he said. We reached the subway station. This is your station?" he asked. I nodded.

---

1 **the corners of his mouth:** os cantos da boca • 2 **dread:** terror • 3 **cheerfully:** alegremente • 4 **it's none of my business:** não é da minha conta • 5 **rough:** duro

I took one step down. "Damn[1]!" he said, suddenly. I looked up at him. He grinned again. "Damn it if I didn't leave all my money home. You ain't got a dollar on you, have you? Just for a couple of days, is all."

All at once something inside gave and threatened[2] to come pouring out of me. I didn't hate him any more. I felt that in another moment I'd start crying like a child.

"Sure," I said. "Don't sweat[3]." I looked in my wallet and didn't have a dollar, I only had a five. "Here," I said. That hold you[4]?"

He didn't look at it—he didn't want to look at it. A terrible, closed look came over his face, as though he were keeping the number on the bill a secret from him and me. "Thanks," he said, and now he was dying to see me go. "Don't worry about Sonny. Maybe I'll write him or something."

"Sure," I said. "You do that. So long[5]."

"Be seeing you," he said. I went on down the steps.

And I didn't write Sonny or send him anything for a long time. When I finally did, it was just after my little girl died, he wrote me back a letter which made me feel like a bastard.

Here's what he said:

Dear brother,

You don't know how much I needed to hear fom you. I wanted to write you many a time but I dug[6] how much I must have hurt you and so I didn't write. But now I feel like a man who's been trying to climb up out of some deep, real deep and

---

1 **damn!:** maldita seja! • 2 **threatened:** ameaçava • 3 **don't sweat:** não se preocupe • 4 **that hold you?:** adianta?; ajuda? • 5 **so long:** até logo • 6 **I dug:** entendia

funky hole and just saw the sun up there, outside. I got to get outside.

I can't tell you much about how I got here. I mean I don't know how to tell you. I guess I was afraid of something or I was trying to escape from something and you know I have never been very strong in the head (smile). I'm glad Mama and Daddy are dead and can't see what's happened to their son and I swear[1] if I'd known what I was doing I would never have hurt you so, you and a lot of other fine people who were nice to me and who believed in me.

I don't want you to think it had anything to do with me being a musician. It's more than that. Or maybe less than that. I can't get anything straight in my head[2] down here and I try not to think about what's going to happen to me when I get outside again. Sometime I think I'm going to flip[3] and *never* get outside and sometime I think I'll come straight back. I tell you one thing, though, I'd rather blow my brains out[4] than go through this again. But that's what they all say, so they tell me[5]. If I tell you when I'm coming to New York and if you could meet me, I sure would appreciate it. Give my love to Isabel and the kids and I was sure sorry to hear about little Gracie. I wish I could be like Mama and say the Lord's will be done[6], but I don't know it seems to me that trouble is the one thing that never does get stopped and I don't know what good it does to blame it on[7] the Lord. But maybe it does some good if you believe it.

Your brother,
Sonny

1 **I swear:** eu juro • 2 **I can't get anything straight in my head:** não consigo pensar direito • 3 **I'm going to flip:** vou ficar maluco • 4 **blow my brains out:** meu cérebro vai explodir • 5 **so they tell me:** eles dizem • 6 **the Lord's will be done:** é a vontade do Senhor • 7 **to blame it on:** jogar a culpa em

Then I kept in constant touch with him and I sent him whatever I could and I went to meet him when he came back to New York. When I saw him many things I thought I had forgotten came flooding back to me[1]. This was because I had begun, finally, to wonder about[2] Sonny, about the life that Sonny lived inside. This life, whatever it was, had made him older and thinner and it had deepened the distant stillness[3] in which he had always moved. He looked very unlike[4] my baby brother. Yet, when he smiled, when we shook hands, the baby brother I'd never known looked out from the depths[5] of his private life, like an animal waiting to be coaxed[6] into the light.

"How you been keeping?" he asked me.

"All right And you?"

"Just fine." He was smiling all over his face. "It's good to see you again."

"It's good to see you."

The seven years' difference in our ages lay between us like a chasm[7]: I wondered if these years would ever operate between us as a bridge. I was remembering, and it made it hard to catch my breath[8], that I had been there when he was born; and I had heard the first words he had ever spoken. When he started to walk, he walked from our mother straight to me[9]. I caught him just before he fell when he took the first steps he ever took in this world.

"How's Isabel?"

---

1 **came flooding back to me:** se amontoaram em minha memória • 2 **to wonder about:** a questionar-me sobre • 3 **stillness:** calma • 4 **unlike:** diferente • 5 **depths:** profundidades • 6 **waiting to be coaxed:** esperando ser convencido • 7 **chasm:** abismo • 8 **to catch my breath:** respirar • 9 **straight to me:** direto para mim

"Just fine. She's dying to see you."

"And the boys?"

"They're fine, too. They're anxious to see their uncle."

"Oh, come on. You know they don't remember me."

"Are you kidding[1]? Of course they remember you."

He grinned again. We got into a taxi. We had a lot to say to each other, far too much to know how to begin.

As the taxi began to move, I asked, "You still want to go to India?"

He laughed. "You still remember that. Hell, no. This place is Indian enough for me."

"It used to belong to them," I said.

And he laughed again. "They damn sure knew what they were doing when they got rid of it[2]."

Years ago, when he was around fourteen, he'd been all hipped on[3] the idea of going to India. He read books about people sitting on rocks, naked, in all kinds of weather, but mostly bad, naturally, and walking barefoot[4] through hot coals[5] and arriving at wisdom[6]. I used to say that it sounded to me as though they were getting away from wisdom as fast as they could. I think he sort of looked down on me[7] for that.

"Do you mind," he asked, "if we have the driver drive alongside the park? On the west side—I haven't seen the city in so long."

"Of course not," I said. I was afraid that I might sound as

---

1 **are you kidding?:** você está brincando? • 2 **they got rid of it:** se desfizeram dele • 3 **he'd been all hipped on:** estava obcecado com • 4 **barefoot:** descalço • 5 **coals:** carvão • 6 **wisdom:** sabedoria • 7 **looked down on me:** me menosprezava

though I were humoring him¹, but I hoped he wouldn't take it that way.

So we drove along, between the green of the park and the stony, lifeless elegance of hotels and apartment buildings, toward the vivid, killing streets of our childhood. These streets hadn't changed, though housing projects² jutted up³ out of them now like rocks in the middle of a boiling sea. Most of the houses in which we had grown up had vanished, as had the stores from which we had stolen, the basements⁴ in which we had first tried sex, the rooftops from which we had hurled⁵ tin cans⁶ and bricks⁷. But houses exactly like the houses of our past yet⁸ dominated the landscape, boys exactly like the boys we once had been found themselves smothering⁹ in these houses, came down into the streets for light and air and found themselves encircled by disaster. Some escaped the trap, most didn't. Those who got out always left something of themselves behind, as some animals amputate a leg and leave it in the trap. It might be said, perhaps, that I had escaped, after all, I was a school teacher; or that Sonny had, he hadn't lived in Harlem for years. Yet, as the cab moved uptown through streets which seemed, with a rush, to darken with dark people, and as I covertly¹⁰ studied Sonny's face, it came to me¹¹ that what we both were seeking through our separate cab windows was that part of ourselves which had

---

1 **humoring him:** seguindo a corrente • 2 **housing projects:** projetos habitacionais • 3 **jutted up:** sobressaíam • 4 **basements:** porões • 5 **we had hurled:** havíamos atirado • 6 **tin cans:** latas • 7 **bricks:** tijolos • 8 **yet:** ainda • 9 **found themselves smothering:** se asfixiavam • 10 **covertly:** secretamente • 11 **it came to me:** me ocorreu

been left behind. It's always at the hour of trouble and confrontation that the missing member aches[1].

We hit 110th Street and started rolling up Lenox Avenue. And I'd known this avenue all my life, but it seemed to me again, as it had seemed on the day I'd first heard about Sonny's trouble, filled with a hidden menace which was its very breath of life.

"We almost there," said Sonny.

"Almost." We were both too nervous to say anything more.

We live in a housing project. It hasn't been up long[2]. A few days after it was up it seemed uninhabitably new, now, of course, it's already rundown[3]. It looks like a parody of the good, clean, faceless[4] life—God knows the people who live in it do their best to make it a parody. The beat-looking[5] grass lying around isn't enough to make their lives green, the hedges[6] will never hold out[7] the streets, and they know it. The big windows fool no one[8], they aren't big enough to make space out of no space. They don't bother with[9] the windows, they watch the TV screen instead. The playground is most popular with the children who don't play at jacks[10], or skip rope[11], or roller skate, or swing[12], and they can be found in it after dark. We moved in partly because it's not too far from where I teach, and partly for the kids; but it's really just

---

1 **the missing member aches:** o membro amputado dói • 2 **it hasn't been up long:** não foi construído há muito tempo • 3 **rundown:** muito deteriorado • 4 **faceless:** anônima • 5 **beat-looking:** descuidada • 6 **hedges:** cerca viva • 7 **will never hold out:** nunca esconderão • 8 **fool no one:** não enganam ninguém • 9 **they don't bother with:** não se preocupam com • 10 **jacks:** jogo infantil • 11 **skip rope:** pular corda • 12 **swing:** balançar-se

like the houses in which Sonny and I grew up. The same things happen, they'll have the same things to remember. The moment Sonny and I started into the house I had the feeling that I was simply bringing him back into the danger he had almost died trying to escape.

Sonny has never been talkative. So I don't know why I was sure he'd be dying to talk to me when supper was over the first night. Everything went fine, the oldest boy remembered him, and the youngest boy liked him, and Sonny had remembered to bring something for each of them; and Isabel, who is really much nicer than I am, more open and giving[1], had gone to a lot of trouble about dinner and was genuinely[2] glad to see him. And she's always been able to tease[3] Sonny in a way that I haven't. It was nice to see her face so vivid again and to hear her laugh and watch her make Sonny laugh. She wasn't, or, anyway, she didn't seem to be, at all uneasy[4] or embarrassed[5]. She chatted as though there were no subject which had to be avoided and she got Sonny past his first, faint stiffness[6]. And thank God she was there, for I was filled with that icy dread again. Everything I did seemed awkward[7] to me, and everything I said sounded freighted[8] with hidden meaning. I was trying to remember everything I'd heard about dope[9] addiction and I couldn't help[10] watching Sonny for signs. I wasn't doing it out of malice[11]. I was trying to find out something about my brother. I was dying to hear him tell me he was safe.

---

1 **giving:** generosa • 2 **genuinely:** de verdade • 3 **to tease:** irritar • 4 **uneasy:** inquieta • 5 **embarrassed:** incomodada • 6 **faint stiffness:** ligeira síncope • 7 **awkward:** torpe • 8 **freighted:** carregado • 9 **dope:** droga • 10 **I couldn't help:** não podia evitar • 11 **out of malice:** maliciosamente

"Safe!" my father grunted[1], whenever Mama suggested trying to move to a neighborhood which might be safer for children. "Safe, hell! Ain't no place safe for kids, nor nobody."

He always went on like this, but he wasn't, ever, really as bad as he sounded, not even[2] on weekends, when he got drunk. As a matter of fact, he was always on the lookout[3] for "something a little better," but he died before he found it. He died suddenly, during a drunken weekend in the middle of the war, when Sonny was fifteen. He and Sonny hadn't ever got on too well[4]. And this was partly because Sonny was the apple of his father's eye[5]. It was because he loved Sonny so much and was frightened for him, that he was always fighting with him. It doesn't do any good to fight with Sonny. Sonny just moves back[6], inside himself, where he can't be reached. But the principal reason that they never hit it off[7] is that they were so much alike. Daddy was big and rough[8] and loud-talking, just the opposite of Sonny, but they both had—that same privacy.

Mama tried to tell me something about this, just after Daddy died. I was home on leave[9] from the army.

This was the last time I ever saw my mother alive. Just the same[10], this picture gets all mixed up[11] in my mind with pictures I had of her when she was younger. The way I always see her is the way she used to be on a Sunday afternoon, say,

---

1 **grunted:** grunhia • 2 **not even:** nem sequer • 3 **on the lookout:** à caça • 4 **hadn't ever got on too well:** nunca haviam se dado muito bem • 5 **the apple of his father's eye:** a menina dos olhos do pai • 6 **moves back:** retrai-se • 7 **hit it off:** combinavam • 8 **rough:** duro; rude • 9 **on leave:** de licença • 10 **just the same:** todavia • 11 **gets all mixed up:** se mistura

when the old folks[1] were talking after the big Sunday dinner. I always see her wearing pale blue. She'd be sitting on the sofa. And my father would be sitting in the easy chair[2], not far from her. And the living room would be full of church folks and relatives[3]. There they sit, in chairs all around the living room, and the night is creeping up[4] outside, but nobody knows it yet. You can see the darkness growing against the windowpanes[5] and you hear the street noises every now and again[6], or maybe the jangling beat of a tambourine[7] from one of the churches close by[8], but it's real quiet in the room. For a moment nobody's talking, but every face looks darkening, like the sky outside. And my mother rocks[9] a little from the waist, and my father's eyes are closed. Everyone is looking at something a child can't see. For a minute they've forgotten the children. Maybe a kid is lying on the rug[10], half asleep. Maybe somebody's got a kid in his lap[11] and is absent-mindedly stroking[12] the kid's head. Maybe there's a kid, quiet and big-eyed, curled up[13] in a big chair in the corner. The silence, the darkness coming, and the darkness in the faces frightens the child obscurely. He hopes that the hand which strokes his forehead will never stop—will never die. He hopes that there will never come a time when the old folks won't be sitting around the living room, talking about where they've come from, and what they've seen, and what's happened to them and their kinfolk[14].

1 **old folks:** os mais velhos • 2 **easy chair:** poltrona • 3 **relatives:** parentes • 4 **the night is creeping up:** a noite cai discretamente • 5 **windowpanes:** vidraças • 6 **every now and again:** de vez em quando • 7 **the jangling beat of a tambourine:** o ritmo metálico de um tamborim • 8 **close by:** próximo • 9 **rocks:** se equilibra • 10 **rug:** tapete • 11 **lap:** colo • 12 **absent-mindedly stroking:** acariciando distraidamente • 13 **curled up:** enroscado • 14 **kinfolk:** parentes

But something deep and watchful[1] in the child knows that this is bound to end[2], is already ending. In a moment someone will get up and turn on the light. Then the old folks will remember the children and they won't talk any more that day. And when light fills the room, the child is filled with darkness. He knows that every time this happens he's moved just a little closer to that darkness outside. The darkness outside is what the old folks have been talking about. It's what they've come from. It's what they endure[3]. The child knows that they won't talk any more because if he knows too much about what's happened to *them*, he'll know too much too soon, about what's going to happen to *him*.

The last time I talked to my mother, I remember I was restless[4]. I wanted to get out and see Isabel. We weren't married then and we had a lot to straighten out between us.

There Mama sat, in black[5], by the window. She was humming[6] an old church song. *Lord, you brought me from a long ways off.* Sonny was out somewhere. Mama kept watching the streets.

"I don't know," she said, "if I'll ever see you again, after you go off from here. But I hope you'll remember the things I tried to teach you."

"Don't talk like that," I said, and smiled. "You'll be here a long time yet."

She smiled, too, but she said nothing. She was quiet for a long time. And I said, "Mama, don't you worry about

---

1 **watchful:** vigilante • 2 **is bound to end:** acabará cedo ou tarde • 3 **they endure:** suportam • 4 **restless:** inquieto • 5 **in black:** vestida de negro • 6 **she was humming:** cantarolava

nothing. I'll be writing all the time, and you be getting[1] the checks...."

"I want to talk to you about your brother," she said, suddenly. "If anything happens to me he ain't going to have[2] nobody to look out for him[3]."

"Mama," I said, "ain't nothing going to happen to you or Sonny. Sonny's all right. He's a good boy and he's got good sense[4]."

"It ain't a question of his being a good boy," Mama said, "nor of his having good sense. It ain't only the bad ones, nor yet the dumb ones[5] that gets sucked under[6]." She stopped, looking at me. "Your Daddy once had a brother," she said, and she smiled in a way that made me feel she was in pain. "You didn't never know that, did you?"

"No," I said, "I never knew that," and I watched her face.

"Oh, yes," she said, "your Daddy had a brother." She looked out of the window again. "I know you never saw your Daddy cry. But *I* did—many a time, through all these years."

I asked her, "What happened to his brother? How come nobody's ever talked about him?"

This was the first time I ever saw my mother look old.

"His brother got killed," she said, "when he was just a little younger than you are now. I knew him. He was a fine boy. He was maybe a little full of the devil, but he didn't mean nobody no harm[7]."

---

1 **you be getting:** você receberá • 2 **he ain't going to have (he isn't going to):** não vai ter • 3 **nobody to look out for him:** ninguém que olhe por ele • 4 **good sense:** bom senso • 5 **the dumb ones:** os tontos • 6 **gets sucked under:** se deixam arrastar • 7 **he didn't mean nobody no harm:** nunca desejou mal a ninguém

Then she stopped and the room was silent, exactly as it had sometimes been on those Sunday afternoons. Mama kept looking out into the streets.

"He used to have a job in the mill[1]," she said, "and, like all young folks, he just liked to perform[2] on Saturday nights. Saturday nights, him and your father would drift around[3] to different place, go to dances and things like that, or just sit around with people they knew, and your father's brother would sing, he had a fine voice, and play along with himself on his guitar. Well, this particular Saturday night, him and your father was coming home from some place, and they were both a little drunk and there was a moon that night, it was bright like day. Your father's brother was feeling kind of good, and he was whistling[4] to himself, and he had his guitar slung[5] over his shoulder. They was coming down a hill and beneath them was a road that turned off from the highway[6]. Well, your father's brother, being always kind of frisky[7], decided to run down this hill, and he did, with that guitar banging and clanging[8] behind him, and he ran across the road, and he was making water[9] behind a tree. And your father was sort of amused at him[10] and he was still coming down the hill, kind of slow. Then he heard a car motor and that same minute his brother stepped from behind the tree, into the road, in the moonlight. And he started to cross the road. And your father started to run down the hill, he says he

---

1 **mill:** fábrica • 2 **to perform:** atuar • 3 **would drift around:** saíam por aí • 4 **he was whistling:** assoviava • 5 **slung:** pendurada • 6 **that turned off from the highway:** que saía da estrada • 7 **frisky:** travesso • 8 **banging and clanging:** golpeando e fazendo barulho • 9 **he was making water:** estava urinando • 10 **amused at him:** o divertia

don't know why. This car was full of white men. They was all drunk, and when they seen your father's brother they let out a great whoop and holler[1] and they aimed[2] the car straight at him. They was having fun, they just wanted to scare him, the way they do sometimes, you know. But they was drunk. And I guess the boy, being drunk, too, and scared, kind of lost his head. By the time he jumped it was too late. Your father says he heard his brother scream when the car rolled over him[3], and he heard the wood of that guitar when it give[4], and he heard them strings[5] go flying, and he heard them white men shouting, and the car kept on a-going and it ain't stopped till this day. And, time your father got down the hill, his brother weren't nothing but blood and pulp[6]."

Tears were gleaming[7] on my mother's face. There wasn't anything I could say.

"He never mentioned it," she said, "because I never let him mention it before you children. Your Daddy was like a crazy man that night and for many a night thereafter. He says he never in his life seen anything as dark as that road after the lights of that car had gone away. Weren't nothing, weren't nobody on that road, just your Daddy and his brother and that busted[8] guitar. Oh, yes. Your Daddy never did really get right again. Till the day he died he weren't sure but that every white man he saw was the man that killed his brother."

She stopped and took out her handkerchief and dried her eyes and looked at me.

---

1 **they let out a great whoop and holler:** soltaram gritos e grunhidos • 2 **they aimed:** dirigiram • 3 **rolled over him:** rolou sobre ele • 4 **when it give:** quando cedeu • 5 **strings:** cordas • 6 **blood and pulp:** sangue e polpa • 7 **were gleaming:** cintilavam • 8 **busted:** esmagada

"I ain't telling you all this," she said, "to make you scared or bitter[1] or to make you hate nobody. I'm telling you this because you got a brother. And the world ain't changed."

I guess I didn't want to believe this. I guess she saw this in my face. She turned away from me, toward the window again, searching those streets.

"But I praise[2] my Redeemer[3]," she said at last, "that He called your Daddy home before me. I ain't saying it to throw no flowers at myself, but, I declare, it keeps me from feeling too cast down[4] to know I helped your father get safely through this world. Your father always acted like he was the roughest, strongest man on earth. And everybody took him to be like that. But if he hadn't had *me* there—to see his tears!"

She was crying again. Still[5], I couldn't move. I said, "Lord, Lord, Mama, I didn't know it was like that."

"Oh, honey," she said, "there's a lot that you don't know. But you are going to find it out." She stood up from the window and came over to me. "You got to hold on to[6] your brother," she said, "and don't let him fall, no matter what it looks like is happening to him and no matter how evil you gets with him. You going to be evil with him many a time. But don't you forget what I told you, you hear?"

"I won't forget," I said. "Don't you worry, I won't forget. I won't let nothing happen to Sonny."

My mother smiled as though[7] she were amused at something she saw in my face. Then, "You may not be able to stop nothing from happening. But you got to let him know you's *there*."

---

1 **bitter:** amargo • 2 **I praise:** louvado seja • 3 **Redeemer:** Redentor • 4 **cast down:** desanimado • 5 **still:** ainda assim • 6 **to hold on to:** apoiar • 7 **as though:** como se

Two days later I was married, and then I was gone. And I had a lot of things on my mind and I pretty well forgot my promise to Mama until I got shipped home on a special furlough[1] for her funeral.

And, after the funeral, with just Sonny and me alone in the empty kitchen, I tried to find out something about him.

"What do you want to do?" I asked him.

"I'm going to be a musician," he said.

For[2] he had graduated, in the time I had been away, from dancing to the juke box to finding out who was playing what, and what they were doing with it, and he had bought himself a set of drums.

"You mean, you want to be a drummer?" I somehow had the feeling that being a drummer might be all right for other people but not for my brother Sonny.

"I don't think," he said, looking at me very gravely, "that I'll ever be a good drummer. But I think I can play a piano."

I frowned[3]. I'd never played the role of the older brother quite so seriously before, had scarcely[4] ever, in fact, *asked* Sonny a damn thing. I sensed myself in the presence of something I didn't really know how to handle[5], didn't understand. So I made my frown a little deeper as I asked: "What kind of musician do you want to be?"

He grinned. "How many kinds do you think there are?"

"Be *serious*," I said.

He laughed, throwing his head back, and then looked at me. "I *am* serious."

---

1 **furlough:** licença • 2 **for:** porque • 3 **I frowned:** franzi o cenho • 4 **scarcely:** apenas • 5 **to handle:** manejar

"Well, then, for Christ's sake[1], stop kidding around and answer a serious question. I mean, do you want to be a concert pianist, you want to play classical music and all that, or—or what?" Long before I finished he was laughing again. "For Christ's *sake,* Sonny!"

He sobered[2], but with difficulty. "I'm sorry. But you sound so—*scared!*" and he was off again[3].

"Well, you may think it's funny now, baby, but it's not going to be so funny when you have to make your living at it[4], let me tell you *that.*" I was furious because I knew he was laughing at me and I didn't know why.

"No," he said, very sober now, and afraid, perhaps, that he'd hurt me, "I don't want to be a classical pianist. That isn't what interests me. I mean"—he paused, looking hard at me[5], as though his eyes would help me to understand, and then gestured helplessly[6], as though perhaps his hand would help—"I mean, I'll have a lot of studying to do, and I'll have to study *everything,* but, I mean, I want to play *with*—jazz musicians." He stopped. "I want to play jazz," he said.

Well, the word had never before sounded as heavy, as real, as it sounded that afternoon in Sonny's mouth. I just looked at him and I was probably frowning a real frown by this time. I simply couldn't see why on earth he'd want to spend his time hanging around nightclubs, clowning around on bandstands[7], while people pushed each other around a dance floor.

---

1 **for Christ's sake:** pelo amor de Deus • 2 **he sobered:** tranquilizou-se • 3 **he was off again:** começou de novo • 4 **make your living at it:** ganhar a vida com isso • 5 **looking hard at me:** olhando-me fixamente • 6 **helplessly:** desamparadamente • 7 **clowning around on bandstands:** se fazendo de bobo nos bastidores

It seemed—beneath him¹, somehow. I had never thought about it before, had never been forced to, but I suppose I had always put jazz musicians in a class with what Daddy called "good-time people²."

"Are you *serious?*"

"Hell, *yes*, I'm serious."

He looked more helpless than ever, and annoyed, and deeply hurt.

I suggested, helpfully³: "You mean—like Louis Armstrong?"

His face closed as though I'd struck him⁴. "No. I'm not talking about none of that old-time, down home crap⁵."

"Well, look, Sonny, I'm sorry, don't get mad⁶. I just don't altogether get it⁷, that's all. Name somebody—you know, a Jazz musician you admire."

"Bird."

"Who?"

"Bird! Charlie Parker! Don't they teach you nothing in the goddamn army?"

I lit a cigarette. I was surprised and then a little amused to discover that I was trembling. "I've been out of touch⁸," I said. "You'll have to be patient with me. Now. Who's this Parker character?"

"He's just one of the greatest Jazz musicians alive," said Sonny, sullenly⁹, his hands in his pockets, his back to me.

---

1 **beneath him:** indigno dele • 2 **good-time people:** gente de bem com a vida • 3 **helpfully:** amavelmente • 4 **I'd struck him:** o tivesse agredido • 5 **down home crap:** bosta tradicional • 6 **don't get mad:** não se irrite • 7 **I just don't altogether get it:** não consigo entendê-lo • 8 **I've been out of touch:** estou por fora • 9 **sullenly:** de mau humor

"Maybe *the* greatest," he added, bitterly[1], "that's probably why *you* never heard of him."

"All right," I said, "I'm ignorant. I'm sorry. I'll go out and buy all the cat's[2] records right away[3], all right?"

"It don't," said Sonny, with dignity, "make any difference to me[4]. I don't care what you listen to. Don't do me no favors."

I was beginning to realize that I'd never seen him so upset[5] before. With another part of my mind I was thinking that this would probably turn out to be one of those things kids go through and that I shouldn't make it seem important by pushing it too hard[6]. Still, I didn't think it would do any harm to ask: "Doesn't all this take a lot of time? Can you make a living at it?"

He turned back to me and half leaned[7], half sat, on the kitchen table. "Everything takes time," he said, "and—well, yes, sure, I can make a living at it. But what I don't seem to be able to make you understand is that it's the only thing I *want* to do."

"Well, Sonny," I said, gently[8], "you know people can't always do exactly what they *want* to do—"

"No, I don't know that," said Sonny, surprising me. "I think people *ought* to do what they want to do, what else are they alive for?"

"You getting to be a big boy," I said desperately, "it's time you started thinking about your future."

---

1 **bitterly:** com ressentimento • 2 **cat:** criatura • 3 **right away:** agora mesmo • 4 **it don't make any difference to me:** para mim dá na mesma • 5 **upset:** chateado • 6 **by pushing it too hard:** insistindo muito • 7 **half leaned:** meio inclinado • 8 **gently:** com delicadeza

"I'm thinking about my future," said Sonny, grimly. "I think about it all the time."

I gave up[1]. I decided, if he didn't change his mind[2], that we could always talk about it later. "In the meantime[3]," I said, "you got to finish school." We had already decided that he'd have to move in[4] with Isabel and her folks. I knew this wasn't the ideal arrangement[5] because Isabel's folks are inclined to be dicty[6] and they hadn't especially wanted Isabel to marry me. But I didn't know what else to do. "And we have to get you fixed up[7] at Isabel's."

There was a long silence. He moved from the kitchen table to the window. "That's a terrible idea. You know it yourself."

"Do you have a *better* idea?"

He just walked up and down the kitchen for a minute. He was as tall as I was. He had started to shave. I suddenly had the feeling that I didn't know him at all.

He stopped at the kitchen table and picked up my cigarettes. Looking at me with a kind of mocking, amused defiance[8], he put one between his lips. "You mind?"

"You smoking already?"

He lit the cigarette and nodded, watching me through the smoke. "I just wanted to see if I'd have the courage to smoke in front of you." He grinned and blew a great cloud of smoke to the ceiling. "It was easy." He looked at my face. "Come on, now. I bet you was smoking at my age, tell the truth."

---

1 **I gave up:** desisti • 2 **if he didn't change his mind:** se ele não mudasse de ideia • 3 **in the meantime:** nesse meio-tempo; enquanto isso • 4 **to move in:** mudar-se • 5 **arrangement:** solução • 6 **dicty:** elitistas • 7 **get you fixed up:** instalar-se • 8 **defiance:** rebeldia

I didn't say anything but the truth was on my face, and he laughed. But now there was something very strained[1] in his laugh. "Sure. And I bet that ain't all you was doing."

He was frightening me a little. "Cut the crap[2]," I said. "We already decided that you was going to go and live at Isabel's. Now what's got into you all of a sudden[3]?"

"*You* decided it," he pointed out[4]. "*I* didn't decide nothing." He stopped in front of me, leaning against the stove[5], arms loosely folded. "Look, brother. I don't want to stay in Harlem no more, I really don't." He was very earnest[6]. He looked at me, then over toward the kitchen window. There was something in his eyes I'd never seen before, some thoughtfulness[7], some worry all his own. He rubbed[8] the muscle of one arm. "It's time I was getting out of here."

"Where do you want to *go,* Sonny?"

"I want to join the army. Or the navy, I don't care. If I say I'm old enough, they'll believe me."

Then I got mad. It was because I was so scared. "You must be crazy. You goddamn fool, what the hell do you want to go and join the *army* for?"

"I just told you. To get out of Harlem."

"Sonny, you haven't even finished *school*. And if you really want to be a musician, how do you expect to study if you're in the *army*?"

He looked at me, trapped, and in anguish. "There's ways[9].

---

1 **strained:** tenso • 2 **cut the crap:** larga de bobagem • 3 **what's got into you all of a sudden?:** o que deu em você de repente? • 4 **he pointed out:** indicou • 5 **stove:** fogão • 6 **earnest:** sério • 7 **thoughtfulness:** preocupação • 8 **he rubbed:** esfregou • 9 **there's ways:** há maneiras

SONNY'S BLUES

I might be able to work out some kind of deal[1]. Anyway, I'll have the G.I. Bill[2] when I come out."

"*If* you come out." We stared at each other. "Sonny, please. Be reasonable. I know the setup[3] is far from perfect. But we got to do the best we can."

"I ain't learning nothing in school," he said. "Even when I go." He turned away from me and opened the window and threw his cigarette out into the narrow alley[4]. I watched his back. "At least, I ain't learning nothing you'd want me to learn." He slammed[5] the window so hard I thought the glass would fly out[6], and turned back to me. "And I'm sick of the stink[7] of these garbage cans[8]!"

"Sonny," I said, "I know how you feel. But if you don't finish school now, you're going to be sorry later that you didn't." I grabbed him by the shoulders. "And you only got another year. It ain't so bad. And I'll come back and I swear I'll help you do *whatever* you want to do. Just try to put up with it[9] till I come back. Will you please do that? For me?"

He didn't answer and he wouldn't look at me.

"Sonny. You hear me?"

He pulled away[10]. "I hear you. But you never hear anything *I* say."

I didn't know what to say to that. He looked out of the window and then back at me. "OK," he said, and sighed[11]. "I'll try."

---

1 **to work out some kind of deal:** chegar a algum tipo de acordo • 2 **G.I. Bill:** lei americana de 1944 que oferecia aos veteranos da Segunda Guerra Mundial a oportunidade de estudar • 3 **setup:** contexto; situação • 4 **narrow alley:** passagem estreita; beco • 5 **he slammed:** fechou de golpe • 6 **would fly out:** sairia voando • 7 **stink:** fedor • 8 **garbage cans:** latas de lixo • 9 **to put up with it:** aguentar • 10 **he pulled away:** se afastou • 11 **sighed:** suspirou

Then I said, trying to cheer him up[1] a little. They got a piano at Isabel's. You can practice on it."

And as a matter of fact[2], it did cheer him up for a minute. "That's right," he said to himself. "I forgot that." His face relaxed a little. But the worry, the thoughtfulness, played on it still, the way shadows play on a face which is staring into the fire.

But I thought I'd never hear the end of that piano. At first, Isabel would write me, saying how nice it was that Sonny was so serious about his music and how, as soon as[3] he came in from school, or wherever[4] he had been when he was supposed to be at school, he went straight to that piano and stayed there until suppertime. And, after supper, he went back to that piano and stayed there until everybody went to bed. He was at the piano all day Saturday and all day Sunday. Then he bought a record player[5] and started playing records. He'd play one record over and over again, all day long sometimes, and he'd improvise along with it on the piano. Or he'd play one section of the record, one chord[6], one change, one progression, then he'd do it on the piano. Then back to the record. Then back to the piano.

Well, I really don't know how they stood it[7]. Isabel finally confessed that it wasn't like living with a person at all, it was like living with sound. And the sound didn't make any sense[8] to her, didn't make any sense to any of them—naturally.

---

1 **to cheer him up:** animá-lo • 2 **as a matter of fact:** na realidade • 3 **as soon as:** assim que • 4 **wherever:** em qualquer lugar • 5 **record player:** toca-discos • 6 **chord:** acorde • 7 **they stood it:** o suportaram • 8 **didn't make any sense:** não fazia sentido

SONNY'S BLUES

They began, in a way, to be afflicted by this presence that was living in their home. It was as though Sonny were some sort of god, or monster. He moved in an atmosphere which wasn't like theirs at all. They fed him[1] and he ate, he washed himself, he walked in and out of their door; he certainly wasn't nasty[2] or unpleasant or rude[3]. Sonny isn't any of those things; but it was as though he were all wrapped up[4] in some cloud, some fire, some vision all his own; and there wasn't any way to reach him[5].

At the same time, he wasn't really a man yet, he was still a child, and they had to watch out for him in all kinds of ways. They certainly couldn't throw him out[6]. Neither did they dare[7] to make a great scene about that piano because even they dimly[8] sensed, as I sensed, from so many thousands of miles away, that Sonny was at that piano playing for his life.

But he hadn't been going to school. One day a letter came from the school board[9] and Isabel's mother got it—there had, apparently, been other letters but Sonny had torn them up[10]. This day, when Sonny came in, Isabel's mother showed him the letter and asked where he'd been spending his time. And she finally got it out of him that he'd been down in Greenwich Village[11], with musicians and other characters[12], in a white girl's apartment. And this scared her and she started to scream at him and what came up, once she began—though

---

1 **they fed him:** o alimentaram • 2 **nasty:** desagradável • 3 **rude:** grosseiro • 4 **wrapped up:** envolto; enrolado • 5 **to reach him:** de chegar a ele • 6 **throw him out:** expulsá-lo • 7 **neither did they dare:** também não se atreviam • 8 **dimly:** sutilmente • 9 **the school board:** o conselho escolar • 10 **had torn them up:** as rasgara • 11 **Greenwich Village:** bairro de Nova York conhecido por seu ambiente boêmio e artístico • 12 **characters:** personagens

she denies it[1] to this day—was what sacrifices they were making to give Sonny a decent home and how little he appreciated it.

Sonny didn't play the piano that day. By evening, Isabel's mother had calmed down but then there was the old man to deal with[2], and Isabel herself. Isabel says she did her best to be calm but she broke down[3] and started crying. She says she just watched Sonny's face. She could tell, by watching him, what was happening with him. And what was happening was that they penetrated his cloud, they had reached him. Even if their fingers had been a thousand times more gentle than human fingers ever are, he could hardly help feeling that they had stripped him naked[4] and were spitting[5] on that nakedness. For he also had to see that his presence, that music, which was life or death to him, had been torture for them and that they had endured it, not at all for his sake[6], but only for mine. And Sonny couldn't take that. He can take it a little better today than he could then but he's still not very good at it and, frankly, I don't know anybody who is.

The silence of the next few days must have been louder than the sound of all the music ever played since time began. One morning, before she went to work, Isabel was in his room for something and she suddenly realized[7] that all of his records were gone. And she knew for certain that he was gone. And he was. He went as far as the navy would carry him. He finally sent me a postcard from some place in Greece

---

1 **she denies it:** ela nega • 2 **there was the old man to deal with:** ainda tinha que lidar com o velho • 3 **she broke down:** ela não aguentou • 4 **they had stripped him naked:** o deixaram nu • 5 **were spitting:** cuspiram • 6 **not at all for his sake:** não por ele • 7 **realized:** percebeu

and that was the first I knew that Sonny was still alive. I didn't see him any more until we were both back in New York and the war had long been over.

He was a man by then, of course, but I wasn't willing[1] to see it. He came by[2] the house from time to time[3], but we fought almost every time we met. I didn't like the way he carried himself, loose and dreamlike[4] all the time, and I didn't like his friends, and his music seemed to be merely an excuse for the life he led. It sounded just that weird[5] and disordered.

Then we had a fight, a pretty awful fight, and I didn't see him for months. By and by I looked him up[6], where he was living, in a furnished room in the Village, and I tried to make it up[7]. But there were lots of other people in the room and Sonny just lay on his bed, and he wouldn't come downstairs with me, and he treated these other people as though they were his family and I weren't. So I got mad and then he got mad, and then I told him that he might just as well be dead as live the way he was living. Then he stood up and he told me not to worry about him any more in life, that he *was* dead as far as I was concerned[8]. Then he pushed me to the door and the other people looked on as though nothing were happening, and he slammed the door behind me. I stood in the hallway[9], staring at the door. I heard somebody laugh in the room and then the tears came to my eyes. I started down

---

1 **I wasn't willing:** não estava disposto • 2 **he came by:** passava por • 3 **from time to time:** de vez em quando • 4 **the way he carried himself, loose and dreamlike:** como se comportava, relaxado e distraído • 5 **weird:** esquisito • 6 **by and by I looked him up:** em breve procurei por ele • 7 **make it up:** fazer as pazes • 8 **as far as I was concerned:** para mim • 9 **hallway:** corredor

the steps, whistling to keep from[1] crying, I kept whistling to myself, *You going to need me, baby, one of these cold, rainy days.*

    I read about Sonny's trouble in the spring. Little Grace died in the fall. She was a beautiful little girl. But she only lived a little over two years. She died of polio and she suffered. She had a slight[2] fever for a couple of days, but it didn't seem like anything and we just kept her in bed. And we would certainly have called the doctor, but the fever dropped[3], she seemed to be all right. So we thought it had just been a cold. Then, one day, she was up, playing, Isabel was in the kitchen fixing lunch for the two boys when they'd come in from school, and she heard Grace fall down in the living room. When you have a lot of children you don't always start running when one of them falls, unless they start screaming or something. And, this time, Grace was quiet. Yet, Isabel says that when she heard that *thump*[4] and then that silence, something happened in her to make her afraid. And she ran to the living room and there was little Grace on the floor, all twisted up[5], and the reason she hadn't screamed was that she couldn't get her breath[6]. And when she did scream, it was the worst sound, Isabel says, that she'd ever heard in all her life, and she still hears it sometimes in her dreams. Isabel will sometimes wake me up with a low, moaning, strangled sound[7] and I have to be quick to awaken her and hold her to me and where Isabel is weeping[8] against me seems a mortal wound[9].

1 **whistling to keep from crying:** assoviando para não chorar • 2 **slight:** leve • 3 **dropped:** baixou • 4 **thump:** pancada • 5 **twisted up:** enroscada • 6 **she couldn't get her breath:** não conseguia respirar • 7 **a low, moaning, strangled sound:** um gemido baixo e estrangulado • 8 **weeping:** soluçando • 9 **a mortal wound:** uma ferida mortal

I think I may have written Sonny the very day that little Grace was buried¹. I was sitting in the living room in the dark, by myself, and I suddenly thought of Sonny. My trouble made his real.

One Saturday afternoon, when Sonny had been living with us, or, anyway, been in our house, for nearly two weeks, I found myself wandering aimlessly about the living room, drinking from a can of beer, and trying to work up² the courage to search³ Sonny's room. He was out, he was usually out whenever I was home, and Isabel had taken the children to see their grandparents. Suddenly I was standing still⁴ in front of the living room window, watching Seventh Avenue. The idea of searching Sonny's room made me still⁵. I scarcely dared to admit to myself what I'd be searching for. I didn't know what I'd do if I found it. Or if I didn't.

On the sidewalk across from me, near the entrance to a barbecue joint⁶, some people were holding an old-fashioned⁷ revival meeting. The barbecue cook, wearing a dirty white apron⁸, his conked⁹ hair reddish and metallic in the pale sun, and a cigarette between his lips, stood in the doorway, watching them. Kids and older people paused in their errands¹⁰ and stood there, along with some older men and a couple of very tough-looking women who watched everything that happened on the avenue, as though they owned it, or were maybe owned by it. Well, they were watching this, too. The

---

1 **was buried:** foi enterrada • 2 **to work up:** reunir • 3 **to search:** revistar •
4 **I was standing still:** estava parado • 5 **made me still:** me tranquilizava •
6 **barbecue joint:** churrascaria • 7 **old-fashioned:** antiquado • 8 **apron:** avental •
9 **conked:** alisado • 10 **errands:** tarefas

revival was being carried on by three sisters in black, and a brother. All they had were their voices and their Bibles and a tambourine. The brother was testifying[1] and while he testified two of the sisters stood together, seeming to say, amen, and the third sister walked around with the tambourine outstretched[2] and a couple of people dropped coins into it. Then the brother's testimony ended and the sister who had been taking up the collection dumped the coins[3] into her palm and transferred them to the pocket of her long black robe[4]. Then she raised both hands, striking the tambourine against the air, and then against one hand, and she started to sing. And the two other sisters and the brother joined in.

It was strange, suddenly, to watch, though[5] I had been seeing these street meetings all my life. So, of course, had everybody else down there. Yet, they paused and watched and listened and I stood still at the window. *"Tis the old ship of Zion*[6]*,"* they sang, and the sister with the tambourine kept a steady, tangling beat, *"it has rescued many a thousand!"* Not a soul under the sound of their voices was hearing this song for the first time, not one of them had been rescued. Nor had they seen much in the way of rescue work being done around them. Neither did they especially believe in the holiness[7] of the three sisters and the brother, they knew too much about them, knew where they lived, and how. The woman with the tambourine, whose voice dominated the air, whose face was bright with joy, was divided by very little

---

1 **was testifying:** dando testemunho • 2 **outstreched:** estendido • 3 **dumped the coins:** jogou as moedas • 4 **robe:** túnica • 5 **though:** ainda que • 6 **Tis the old ship of Zion:** "Este é o velho navio de Sião", hino cristão de 1889 • 7 **holiness:** santidade

from the woman who stood watching her, a cigarette between her heavy, chapped¹ lips, her hair a cuckoo's nest², her face scarred³ and swollen⁴ from many beatings⁵, and her black eyes glittering like coal⁶. Perhaps they both knew this, which was why, when, as rarely, they addressed each other, they addressed each other as Sister. As the singing filled the air the watching, listening faces underwent a change, the eyes focusing⁷ on something within; the music seemed to soothe a poison out of them⁸; and time seemed, nearly, to fall away from the sullen, belligerent, battered faces, as though they were fleeing⁹ back to their first condition, while dreaming of their last. The barbecue cook half shook his head and smiled, and dropped his cigarette and disappeared into his joint. A man fumbled¹⁰ in his pockets for change and stood holding it in his hand impatiently, as though he had just remembered a pressing appointment¹¹ further up the avenue. He looked furious. Then I saw Sonny, standing on the edge of the crowd. He was carrying a wide, flat notebook with a green cover, and it made him look, from where I was standing, almost like a schoolboy. The coppery¹² sun brought out the copper in his skin, he was very faintly smiling, standing very still. Then the singing stopped, the tambourine turned into a collection plate again. The furious man dropped in his coins and vanished, so did a couple of the women, and Sonny dropped some change in the plate, looking directly at the woman with

---

1 **chapped:** rachado • 2 **a cuckoo's nest:** um ninho de rato • 3 **scarred:** com cicatrizes • 4 **swollen:** inchada • 5 **beatings:** surras • 6 **glittering like coal:** brilhantes como o carvão • 7 **focusing:** focado; centrado • 8 **to soothe a poison out of them:** acalmar um veneno dentro deles • 9 **they were fleeing:** fugiram • 10 **fumbled:** remexia • 11 **a pressing appointment:** um compromisso urgente • 12 **coppery:** cuprífero; semelhante ao cobre

a little smile. He started across the avenue, toward the house. He has a slow, loping walk[1], something like the way Harlem hipsters[2] walk, only he's imposed on this his own half-beat[3]. I had never really noticed it before.

I stayed at the window, both relieved and apprehensive[4]. As Sonny disappeared from my sight, they began singing again. And they were still singing when his key turned in the lock[5].

"Hey," he said.

"Hey, yourself. You want some beer?"

"No. Well, maybe." But he came up to the window and stood beside me, looking out. "What a warm voice," he said.

They were singing *If I could only hear my mother pray*[6] *again!*

"Yes," I said, "and she can sure beat that tambourine."

"But what a terrible song," he said, and laughed. He dropped his notebook on the sofa and disappeared into the kitchen. "Where's Isabel and the kids?"

I think they went to see their grandparents. You hungry?"

"No." He came back into the living room with his can of beer. "You want to come some place with me tonight?"

I sensed, I don't know how, that I couldn't possibly say no. "Sure. Where?"

He sat down on the sofa and picked up[7] his notebook and

---

1 **a slow, loping walk:** uma maneira lenta e trôpega de andar • 2 **hipsters:** termo usado nos anos 1940 para fazer referência aos fãs do jazz moderno, muito popular no princípio dessa década • 3 **half-beat:** médio compasso • 4 **both relieved and apprehensive:** tanto aliviado quanto apreensivo • 5 **lock:** fechadura • 6 **pray:** rezar • 7 **picked up:** pegou

started leafing through it[1]. I'm going to sit in with some fellows[2] in a joint[3] in the Village."

"You mean, you're going to play, tonight?"

That's right" He took a swallow[4] of his beer and moved back to the window. He gave me a sidelong look[5]. "If you can stand it."

"I'll try," I said.

He smiled to himself and we both watched as the meeting across the way broke up[6]. The three sisters and the brother, heads bowed[7], were singing *God be with you till we meet again*. The faces around them were very quiet. Then the song ended. The small crowd dispersed. We watched the three women and the lone[8] man walk slowly up the avenue.

"When she was singing before," said Sonny, abruptly, "her voice reminded me for a minute of what heroin feels like sometimes—when it's in your veins. It makes you feel sort of warm and cool at the same time. And distant. And—and sure." He sipped[9] his beer, very deliberately not looking at me, I watched his face. "It makes you feel—in control. Sometimes you've got to have that feeling."

"Do you?" I sat down slowly in the easy chair.

"Sometimes." He went to the sofa and picked up his notebook again. "Some people do."

"In order," I asked, "to play?" And my voice was very ugly, full of contempt[10] and anger.

---

1 **leafing through it:** folheá-lo • 2 **fellows:** colegas • 3 **joint:** lugar de jogo clandestino • 4 **swallow:** gole • 5 **a sidelong look:** um olhar de lado; de esguelha • 6 **broke up:** terminou • 7 **heads bowed:** cabeças abaixadas • 8 **lone:** solitário • 9 **he sipped:** deu um gole • 10 **contempt:** desprezo

"Well"—he looked at me with great, troubled eyes, as though, in fact, he hoped his eyes would tell me things he could never otherwise say—"they *think* so. And *if* they think so—!"

"And what do *you* think?" I asked.

He sat on the sofa and put his can of beer on the floor. "I don't know," he said, and I couldn't be sure if he were answering my question or pursuing[1] his thoughts. His face didn't tell me. "It's not so much to *play*. It's to *stand* it, to be able to make it at all. On any level." He frowned and smiled: "In order to keep from shaking to pieces[2]."

"But these friends of yours," I said, "they seem to shake themselves to pieces pretty goddamn fast."

"Maybe." He played with the notebook. And something told me that I should curb my tongue[3], that Sonny was doing his best to talk, that I should listen. "But of course you only know the ones that've gone to pieces. Some don't—or at least they haven't *yet* and that's just about all *any* of us can say." He paused. "And then there are some who just live, really, in hell, and they know it and they see what's happening and they go right on[4]. I don't know." He sighed, dropped the notebook, folded[5] his arms. "Some guys, you can tell from the way they play, they on something[6] *all* the time. And you can see that, well, it makes something real for them. But of course," he picked up his beer from the floor and sipped it and put the can down again, "they *want* to, too, you've got to see

---

1 **pursuing:** seguindo • 2 **in order to keep from shaking to pieces:** para evitar desmoronar • 3 **curb my tongue:** morder minha língua • 4 **they go right on:** continuam do mesmo jeito • 5 **folded:** cruzou • 6 **they on something:** estão ligados

that. Even some of them that say they don't—*some,* not all."

"And what about you?" I asked—I couldn't help it[1]. "What about you? Do *you* want to?"

He stood up and walked to the window and remained silent for a long time. Then he sighed. "Me," he said. Then: "While I was downstairs before, on my way here[2], listening to that woman sing, it struck me all of a sudden how much suffering she must have had to go through—to sing like that. It's *repulsive* to think you have to suffer that much."

I said: "But there's no way not to suffer—is there, Sonny?"

"I believe not," he said and smiled, "but that's never stopped anyone from trying." He looked at me. "Has it?" I realized, with this mocking look, that there stood between us, forever, beyond[3] the power of time or forgiveness[4], the fact that I had held silence—so long[5]!—when he had needed human speech to help him. He turned back to the window. "No, there's no way not to suffer. But you try all kinds of ways to keep from drowning[6] in it, to keep on top of it, and to make it seem—well, like *you.* Like you did something, all right, and now you're suffering for it. You know?" I said nothing, "Well you know," he said, impatiently, "why *do* people suffer? Maybe it's better to do something to give it a reason, *any* reason."

"But we just agreed[7]," I said, "that there's no way not to suffer. Isn't it better, then, just to—take it[8]?"

"But nobody just takes it," Sonny cried, "that's what I'm

---

1 **I couldn't help it:** não podia evitar • 2 **on my way here:** vindo para cá • 3 **beyond:** além • 4 **forgiveness:** perdão • 5 **so long:** tanto tempo • 6 **drowning:** afogar-se • 7 **we just agreed:** concordamos • 8 **take it:** aceitá-lo

telling you! *Everybody* tries not to. You're just hung up on[1] the *way* some people try—it's not *your* way!"

The hair on my face began to itch[2], my face felt wet. "That's not true," I said, "that's not true. I don't give a damn[3] what other people do, I don't even care how they suffer. I just care how *you* suffer." And he looked at me. "Please believe me," I said, 'I don't want to see you—die—trying not to suffer."

"I won't," he said, flatly[4], "die trying not to suffer. At least, not any faster than anybody else."

"But there's no need," I said, trying to laugh, "is there? in killing yourself."

I wanted to say more, but I couldn't. I wanted to talk about will power[5] and how life could be—well, beautiful. I wanted to say that it was all within; but was it? or, rather, wasn't that exactly the trouble? And I wanted to promise that I would never fail him again. But it would all have sounded—empty words and lies.

So I made the promise to myself and prayed that I would keep it[6].

"It's terrible sometimes, inside," he said, "that's what's the trouble. You walk these streets, black and funky and cold, and there's not really a living ass[7] to talk to, and there's nothing shaking, and there's no way of getting it out—that storm inside. You can't talk it and you can't make love with it, and when you finally try to get with it and play it, you realize *nobody's* listening. So *you've* got to listen. You got to find a way to listen."

---

1 **you're just hung up on:** você só está imitando • 2 **itch:** coçar • 3 **I don't give a damn:** não estou nem aí • 4 **flatly:** categórico; terminantemente • 5 **will power:** força de vontade • 6 **keep it:** mantê-la • 7 **there's not really a living ass:** não há vivalma

And then he walked away from the window and sat on the sofa again, as though all the wind[1] had suddenly been knocked out of him. "Sometimes you'll do *anything* to play, even cut your mother's throat[2]." He laughed and looked at me. "Or your brother's." Then he sobered. "Or your own." Then: "Don't worry. I'm all right now and I think I'll *be* all right. But I can't forget—where I've been. I don't mean[3] just the physical place I've been, I mean where I've *been*. And *what* I've been."

"What have you been. Sonny?" I asked.

He smiled—but sat sideways[4] on the sofa, his elbow resting on the back, his fingers playing with his mouth and chin[5], not looking at me. I've been something I didn't recognize, didn't know I could be. Didn't know anybody could be." He stopped, looking inward, looking helplessly young, looking old. "I'm not talking about it now because I feel *guilty*[6] or anything like that—maybe it would be better if I did, I don't know. Anyway, I can't really talk about it. Not to you, not to anybody," and now he turned and faced me. "Sometimes, you know, and it was actually when I was most *out* of the world, I felt that I was in it, that I was *with* it, really, and I could play or I didn't really have to *play*, it just came out of me, it was there. And I don't know how I played, thinking about it now, but I know I did awful[7] things, those times, sometimes, to people. Or it wasn't that I *did* anything to them—it was that they weren't real." He picked up the beer can; it was empty; he rolled it between his palms: "And other times—well,

---

1 **wind:** fôlego • 2 **throat:** garganta • 3 **I don't mean:** não quero dizer • 4 **sideways:** de lado • 5 **chin:** queixo • 6 **I feel guilty:** me sinto culpado • 7 **awful:** horrível

I needed a fix[1], needed to find a place to lean[2], I needed to clear a space to *listen*—and I couldn't find it, and I—went crazy, I did terrible things to *me,* I was terrible *for* me." He began pressing the beer can between his hands, I watched the metal begin to give. It glittered, as he played with it, like a knife, and I was afraid he would cut himself, but I said nothing. "Oh well. I can never tell you. I was all by myself[3] at the bottom of something[4], stinking[5] and sweating and crying and shaking, and I smelled it, you know? *my* stink, and I thought I'd die if I couldn't get away from it and yet, all the same[6], I knew that everything I was doing was just locking me in[7] with it. And I didn't know," he paused, still flattening[8] the beer can, "I didn't know, I still *don't* know, something kept telling me that maybe it was good to smell your own stink, but I didn't think that *that* was what I'd been trying to do—and—who can stand it?" and he abruptly dropped the ruined[9] beer can, looking at me with a small, still smile, and then rose, walking to the window as though it were the lodestone rock[10]. I watched his face, he watched the avenue. "I couldn't tell you when Mama died—but the reason I wanted to leave Harlem so bad was to get away from drugs. And then, when I ran away[11], that's what I was running from—really. When I came back, nothing had changed, *I* hadn't changed, I was just—older." And he stopped, drumming[12] with his fingers on the windowpane. The sun had vanished,

---

1 **fix:** solução • 2 **a place to lean:** um lugar para me deitar • 3 **all by myself:** completamente sozinho • 4 **at the bottom of something:** no fundo do poço • 5 **stinking:** fedendo • 6 **all the same:** mesmo assim • 7 **locking me in:** trancando-me • 8 **flattening:** amassando • 9 **ruined:** destroçada • 10 **lodestone rock:** ímã • 11 **I ran away:** fugi • 12 **drumming:** tamborilando

soon darkness would fall. I watched his face. "It can come again," he said, almost as though speaking to himself. Then he turned to me. "It can come again," he repeated. "I just want you to know that"

"All right," I said, at last. "So it can come again. All right."

He smiled, but the smile was sorrowful[1]. "I had to try to tell you," he said.

"Yes," I said. "I understand that."

"You're my brother," he said, looking straight at me, and not smiling at all.

"Yes," I repeated, "yes. I understand that."

He turned back to the window, looking out. "All that hatred[2] down there," he said, "all that hatred and misery and love. It's a wonder it doesn't blow the avenue apart[3]."

We went to the only nightclub on a short, dark street, downtown. We squeezed through the narrow, chattering, jam-packed[4] bar to the entrance of the big room, where the bandstand was. And we stood there for a moment, for the lights were very dim[5] in this room and we couldn't see. Then, "Hello, boy," said a voice and an enormous black man, much older than Sonny or myself, erupted out of all that atmospheric lighting and put an arm around Sonny's shoulder. "I been sitting right here," he said, "waiting for you."

He had a big voice, too, and heads in the darkness turned toward us.

---

1 **sorrowful:** triste • 2 **hatred:** ódio • 3 **it's a wonder it doesn't blow the avenue apart:** é um milagre que não faça a avenida ir pelos ares • 4 **jam-packed:** lotado • 5 **dim:** tênues

Sonny grinned and pulled a little away, and said, "Creole, this is my brother. I told you about him."

Creole shook my hand. "I'm glad to meet you, son," he said, and it was clear that he was glad to meet me *there,* for Sonny's sake. And he smiled, "You got a real musician in *your* family," and he took his arm from Sonny's shoulder and slapped him[1], lightly, affectionately, with the back of his hand.

"Well. Now I've heard it all," said a voice behind us. This was another musician, and a friend of Sonny's, a coal-black, cheerful-looking man, built close to the ground[2]. He immediately began confiding to me[3], at the top of his lungs[4], the most terrible things about Sonny, his teeth gleaming like a lighthouse and his laugh coming up out of him like the beginning of an earthquake[5]. And it turned out that everyone at the bar knew Sonny, or almost everyone; some were musicians, working there, or nearby, or not working, some were simply hangers-on[6], and some were there to hear Sonny play. I was introduced to all of them and they were all very polite to me. Yet, it was clear that, for them, I was only Sonny's brother. Here, I was in Sonny's world. Or, rather: his kingdom[7]. Here, it was not even a question that his veins bore royal blood.

They were going to play soon and Creole installed me, by myself, at a table in a dark corner. Then I watched them, Creole, and the little black man, and Sonny, and the

---

1 **slapped him:** esbofeteou-o • 2 **built close to the ground:** baixo, que não subia um palmo do solo • 3 **began confiding to me:** começou a confiar em mim • 4 **at the top of his lungs:** a plenos pulmões • 5 **earthquake:** terremoto • 6 **hangers-on:** parasitas • 7 **kingdom:** reino

others, while they horsed around[1], standing just below the bandstand. The light from the bandstand spilled just a little short of them[2] and, watching them laughing and gesturing and moving about, I had the feeling that they, nevertheless[3], were being most careful not to step into that circle of light too suddenly: that if they moved into the light too suddenly, without thinking, they would perish in flame[4]. Then, while I watched, one of them, the small, black man, moved into the light and crossed the bandstand and started fooling around[5] with his drums. Then—being funny and being, also, extremely ceremonious—Creole took Sonny by the arm and led him to the piano. A woman's voice called Sonny's name and a few hands started clapping[6]. And Sonny, also being funny and being ceremonious, and so touched[7], I think, that he could have cried, but neither hiding it nor showing it, riding it like a man, grinned, and put both hands to his heart and bowed from the waist.

Creole then went to the bass fiddle[8] and a lean[9], very bright-skinned brown man jumped up on the bandstand and picked up his horn[10]. So there they were, and the atmosphere on the bandstand and in the room began to change and tighten[11]. Someone stepped up to the microphone and announced them. Then there were all kinds of murmurs. Some people at the bar shushed[12] others. The waitress ran

---

1 **they horsed around:** causavam alvoroço • 2 **spilled just a little short of them:** caía a pouca distância deles • 3 **nevertheless:** todavia • 4 **they would perish in flame:** morreriam nas chamas • 5 **fooling around:** brincando • 6 **clapping:** aplaudir • 7 **touched:** emocionado • 8 **bass fiddle:** contrabaixo • 9 **lean:** magro • 10 **horn:** no jazz, qualquer instrumento metálico de sopro • 11 **tighten:** ficar tensa • 12 **shushed:** pediram silêncio

around, frantically getting in the last orders, guys and chicks[1] got closer to each other, and the lights on the bandstand, on the quartet, turned to a kind of indigo[2]. Then they all looked different there. Creole looked about him for the last time, as though he were making certain that all his chickens were in the coop[3], and then he jumped and struck the fiddle. And there they were.

All I know about music is that not many people ever really hear it. And even then, on the rare occasions when something opens within, and the music enters, what we mainly hear, or hear corroborated, are personal, private, vanishing evocations. But the man who creates the music is hearing something else, is dealing with the roar rising from the void[4] and imposing order on it as it hits the air. What is evoked in him, then, is of another order, more terrible because it has no words, and triumphant, too, for that same reason. And his triumph, when he triumphs, is ours. I just watched Sonny's face. His face was troubled, he was working hard, but he wasn't with it. And I had the feeling that, in a way, everyone on the bandstand was waiting for him, both waiting for him and pushing him along. But as I began to watch Creole, I realized that it was Creole who held them all back[5]. He had them on a short rein[6]. Up there, keeping the beat with his whole body, wailing on the fiddle[7], with his eyes half closed, he was listening to everything, but he was listening to Sonny. He was having a dialogue with Sonny. He wanted Sonny

---

1 **chicks:** garotas • 2 **indigo:** índigo (cor entre o azul e o violeta) • 3 **coop:** galinheiro • 4 **is dealing with the roar rising from the void:** está lidando com o rugido que vem do vazio • 5 **held them all back:** continha todos • 6 **he had them on a short rein:** os trazia na rédea curta • 7 **wailing on the fiddle:** gemendo no contrabaixo

to leave the shoreline[1] and strike out for the deep water. He was Sonny's witness that deep water and drowning were not the same thing—he had been there, and he knew. And he wanted Sonny to know. He was waiting for Sonny to do the things on the keys[2] which would let Creole know that Sonny was in the water.

And, while Creole listened, Sonny moved, deep within, exactly like someone in torment. I had never before thought of how awful the relationship must be between the musician and his instrument. He has to fill it, this instrument, with the breath of life, his own. He has to make it do what he wants it to do. And a piano is just a piano. It's made out of so much wood and wires[3] and little hammers[4] and big ones, and ivory[5]. While there's only so much you can do with it, the only way to find this out is to try; to try and make it do everything.

And Sonny hadn't been near a piano for over a year. And he wasn't on much better terms with[6] his life, not the life that stretched before him[7] now. He and the piano stammered[8], started one way, got scared, stopped; started another way, panicked, marked time, started again; then seemed to have found a direction, panicked again, got stuck[9]. And the face I saw on Sonny I'd never seen before. Everything had been burned out of it, and, at the same time, things usually hidden were being burned in, by the fire and fury of the battle which was occurring in him up there.

1 **shoreline:** margem• 2 **keys:** teclas• 3 **wires:** cordas (de piano)• 4 **hammers:** martelos (do piano)• 5 **ivory:** marfim• 6 **he wasn't on much better terms with:** ele não estava muito melhor com• 7 **stretched before him:** se estendia diante dele• 8 **stammered:** balbuciavam• 9 **got stuck:** congelavam

Yet, watching Creole's face as they neared the end of the first set, I had the feeling that something had happened, something I hadn't heard. Then they finished, there was scattered[1] applause, and then, without an instant's warning, Creole started into something else, it was almost sardonic, it was *Am I Blue*. And, as though he commanded[2], Sonny began to play. Something began to happen. And Creole let out the reins. The dry, low, black man said something awful on the drums, Creole answered, and the drums talked back. Then the horn insisted, sweet and high, slightly detached[3] perhaps, and Creole listened, commenting now and then, dry, and driving, beautiful and calm and old. Then they all came together again, and Sonny was part of the family again. I could tell this from his face. He seemed to have found, right there beneath his fingers, a damn brand-new[4] piano. It seemed that he couldn't get over it[5]. Then, for awhile, just being happy with Sonny, they seemed to be agreeing with him that brand-new pianos certainly were a gas[6].

Then Creole stepped forward to remind them that what they were playing was the blues. He hit something in all of them, he hit something in me, myself, and the music tightened and deepened, apprehension began to beat the air. Creole began to tell us what the blues were all about[7]. They were not about anything very new. He and his boys up there were keeping it new, at the risk of ruin, destruction, madness, and death, in order to find new ways to make us listen. For, while

---

1 **scattered:** isolados • 2 **he commanded:** ordenara • 3 **detached:** distante • 4 **brand-new:** novo em folha • 5 **it seemed that he couldn't get over it:** parecia incapaz de dominá-lo • 6 **were a gas:** eram demais • 7 **what the blues were all about:** em que consiste o blues

the tale of how we suffer, and how we are delighted, and how we may triumph is never new, it always must be heard. There isn't any other tale to tell, it's the only light we've got in all this darkness.

And this tale, according to that face, that body, those strong hands on those strings, has another aspect in every country, and a new depth in every generation. Listen, Creole seemed to be saying, listen. Now these are Sonny's blues[1]. He made the little black man on the drums know it, and the bright, brown man on the horn. Creole wasn't trying any longer to get Sonny in the water. He was wishing him Godspeed[2]. Then he stepped back, very slowly, filling the air with the immense suggestion that Sonny speak for himself.

Then they all gathered around[3] Sonny and Sonny played. Every now and again one of them seemed to say, amen. Sonny's fingers filled the air with life, his life. But that life contained so many others. And Sonny went all the way back, he really began with the spare, flat statement[4] of the opening phrase of the song. Then he began to make it his. It was very beautiful because it wasn't hurried[5] and it was no longer a lament. I seemed to hear with what burning he had made it his, with what burning we had yet to make it ours, how we could cease lamenting. Freedom lurked around us[6] and I understood, at last, that he could help us to be free if we would listen, that he would never be free until we did. Yet, there was

---

1 **these are Sonny's blues:** esta é a tristeza de Sonny (jogo de palavras entre as duas acepções da palavra blues: o ritmo musical e tristeza) • 2 **he was wishing him Godspeed:** lhe desejava boa sorte • 3 **they all gathered around Sonny:** se juntaram todos ao redor de Sonny • 4 **flat statement:** declaração contundente • 5 **it wasn't hurried:** não era apressado • 6 **lurked around us:** nos envolvia

no battle in his face now. I heard what he had gone through, and would continue to go through until he came to rest in earth. He had made it his: that long line, of which we knew only Mama and Daddy. And he was giving it back[1], as everything must be given back, so that, passing through death, it can live forever. I saw my mother's face again, and felt, for the first time, how the stones of the road she had walked on must have bruised her feet[2]. I saw the moonlit road[3] where my father's brother died. And it brought something else back to me, and carried me past it, I saw my little girl again and felt Isabel's tears again, and I felt my own tears begin to rise. And I was yet aware[4] that this was only a moment, that the world waited outside, as hungry as a tiger, and that trouble stretched above us, longer than the sky.

Then it was over. Creole and Sonny let out their breath, both soaking wet[5], and grinning. There was a lot of applause and some of it was real. In the dark, the girl came by and I asked her to take drinks to the bandstand. There was a long pause, while they talked up there in the indigo light and after awhile I saw the girl put a Scotch[6] and milk on top of the piano for Sonny. He didn't seem to notice it, but just before they started playing again, he sipped from it and looked toward me, and nodded. Then he put it back on top of the piano. For me, then, as they began to play again, it glowed[7] and shook above my brother's head like the very cup of trembling[8].

---

1 **he was giving it back:** estava devolvendo • 2 **must have bruised her feet:** devem ter machucado os pés • 3 **moonlit road:** estrada iluminada pelo luar • 4 **I was yet aware:** eu estava, contudo, consciente • 5 **soaking wet:** encharcados • 6 **Scotch:** uísque escocês • 7 **it glowed:** brilhou • 8 **the very cup of trembling:** o cálice do furor (referência bíblica)

Jack London
A Piece of Steak

"For Youth was ever youthful. It was only Age that grew old."

BIOGRAFIA
Jack London

O garoto que aprendeu a ler na biblioteca e que acabou escrevendo para adicionar 4 mil acres a um enorme rancho na Califórnia nem sequer soube quem era seu pai. Jack London (1876-1916) é, supostamente, filho do astrólogo William Chaney, que nunca o reconheceu. O que se sabe é que o escritor nasceu em São Francisco, e que sua mãe, Flora Wellman, garantia ter sido casada com Chaney. Seja como for, London nunca foi à escola. Educou-se na biblioteca do bairro e descobriu que queria ser escritor depois de ler uma novela intitulada *Signa* – a história de um camponês italiano sem estudos que se torna compositor de ópera.

Quando completou 17 anos, embarcou na escuna *Sophia Sutherland* e viajou para o Japão. Na volta, os Estados Unidos estavam em crise. Não havia trabalho. E o pouco que havia era suficiente apenas para viver. Nessa época, London chegou a trabalhar de 12 a 18 horas numa fábrica de conservas. Sua vida era tão terrível que foi levado a pedir dinheiro emprestado à sua mãe de criação para comprar uma escuna. Durante algum tempo foi apanhador de ostras, mas não deu certo. Regressou à terra firme e, como não tinha o que comer, o jovem escritor (tinha acabado de completar 18 anos) virou vagabundo, o que o levou à prisão. Passou 30 dias na penitenciária de Buffalo e depois voltou para São Francisco. Frequentou a escola e depois a universidade, mas teve de abandoná-la um ano após matricular-se (com 21 anos) porque não podia pagar. Nunca chegou a se formar.

Nesse mesmo ano, 1897, London esteve à beira da morte. Contraiu escorbuto num navio; escapou por milagre. Em seu regresso a São Francisco decidiu que, para se livrar do trabalho, tinha de escrever e publicar seus textos. Foi assim que começou sua carreira. Pensou em desistir, porém, quando recebeu o cheque por sua primeira história (cinco miseráveis dólares). O seguinte foi de US$ 40. Três anos depois, com somente 24 anos, já ganhava US$ 2.500 por ano por seus contos. Nessa época, continuava sendo socialista (o foi desde os 20 anos até o fim de seus dias) e havia se casado com Bessie Madern, ainda que nenhum dos dois estivesse apaixonado. Casaram porque assim teriam "filhos fortes" – ou isso foi o que London disse. London tinha uma amante (Anna Strunsky), com a qual chegou a escrever uma comédia romântica: *The Kempton-Wace Letters* [As cartas de Kempton-Wace].

Durante esses anos publicou suas célebres histórias, *Chamado selvagem* em 1903 e, três anos depois, *Caninos brancos*, nas quais uma natureza selvagem faz frente ao homem e o sacode até que considere que já teve o suficiente. Naquela época, London tirava a maior parte de suas ideias de notícias dos jornais (foi, inclusive, acusado de plágio por isso). Seis anos antes de morrer, em 1910, London comprou um gigantesco rancho em Glen Ellen (Califórnia). A partir de então começou a escrever de maneira doentia para aumentar o rancho. Acometido por uma estranha enfermidade, morreu em 1916, provavelmente de uma overdose de morfina. Desde então, a teoria de suicídio se mantém. Quando morreu, London deixou cerca de 50 romances e uma biblioteca particular de 15 mil volumes.

LAURA FERNÁNDEZ

APRESENTAÇÃO DO CONTO
A Piece of Steak

Tom King não é mais do que um velho boxeador. Mas houve um tempo em que era uma grande estrela. Um tempo em que fazia tudo pela fama, por algumas doses, pelas mulheres... tudo isso. Mas a idade o consumiu, como o resto, e os dias de glória se converteram numa geladeira vazia. Por isso, tem de voltar a lutar. Porque não sabe ganhar a vida de outra maneira e porque não tem nenhum pedaço de carne para levar à boca, Tom vai lutar contra um tipo chamado Sandel, um jovem neozelandês desconhecido na Austrália, mas que fez nome em seu país natal. Sua mulher lhe diz que não precisa lutar se não quiser, mas Tom quer fazer, tem de fazer. Enquanto vai andando para o combate, recorda como, em outros tempos, ele era a jovem promessa, e Stowsher Bill, a velha glória. Recorda como o fez em pedaços no ringue e então percebe o que foi que realmente reduziu o pobre Bill a pedaços.

Teria Bill jantado aquela noite?

"A Piece of Steak", com "To Build a Fire", é o melhor conto de Jack London. Foi publicado originalmente na revista americana *The Saturday Evening Post*, em novembro de 1909, e London recebeu cerca de US$ 500 por ele. Na época, o autor já era muito conhecido, e o combate entre a insultuosa juventude e a temível idade que se dá na história tinha muito a ver com o momento que vivia. O escritor, autodidata e ambicioso, conhecido como a voz da natureza em seu sentido mais cruel e ao mesmo tempo mais leal, sabia do que estava falando. Tom King vive mal num subúrbio, mas ao menos tem um teto. Houve um tempo em que Jack London não tinha nenhum. A força do conto reside precisamente nisso, em que tudo acontece por alguma razão. É autêntico. E a prosa honesta de London é capaz de elevar um feito cotidiano à categoria de clássico: a breve conversa de Tom com sua mulher antes de sair para o ginásio é um exemplo contundente.

Construído de maneira cronológica e dividido de forma natural em rounds (que têm lugar entre Sandel e Tom King, mas também entre a juventude e a idade), "A Piece of Steak" é uma dessas joias da literatura universal que devem ser lidas pausadamente para que se aprecie a mais firme prosa do autor, que contém os músculos que deviam tecer o corpo de Tom King quando era um garoto e podia encarar Stowsher Bill.

Para resolver questões lexicais, você pode consultar as muitas palavras e expressões traduzidas no rodapé. E para desfrutar da voz (narrativa) de London, esta edição inclui um CD com a versão em áudio da história. Vai perder?

LAURA FERNÁNDEZ

A Piece of Steak

WITH THE LAST MORSEL¹ of bread Tom King wiped² his plate clean of the last particle of flour gravy³ and chewed⁴ the resulting mouthful⁵ in a slow and meditative way. When he arose⁶ from the table, he was oppressed by the feeling that he was distinctly hungry. Yet⁷ he alone had eaten. The two children in the other room had been sent early to bed in order that in sleep they might forget they had gone supperless. His wife had touched nothing, and had sat silently and watched him with solicitous eyes. She was a thin, worn⁸ woman of the working-class, though signs of an earlier prettiness were not wanting⁹ in her face. The flour for the gravy she had borrowed from the neighbour across the hall. The last two ha'pennies¹⁰ had gone to buy the bread.

He sat down by the window on a rickety chair¹¹ that protested under his weight, and quite mechanically he put his pipe in his mouth and dipped into the side pocket of his coat. The absence of any tobacco made him aware of his action, and, with a scowl¹² for his forgetfulness¹³, he put the pipe away¹⁴. His movements were slow, almost hulking¹⁵, as though he were burdened by the heavy weight of his muscles.

1 **morsel:** pedaço• 2 **wiped:** limpou• 3 **flour gravy:** molho de farinha• 4 **chewed:** mastigou• 5 **mouthful:** bocado• 6 **he arose:** levantou• 7 **yet:** contudo• 8 **worn:** cansada; acabada• 9 **were not wanting:** não faltavam• 10 **ha'pennies (half pennies):** centavos• 11 **rickety chair:** cadeira bamba• 12 **with a scowl:** com a testa franzida• 13 **forgetfulness:** memória ruim• 14 **he put the pipe away:** guardou o cachimbo• 15 **hulking:** desajeitados

He was a solid-bodied, stolid-looking[1] man, and his appearance did not suffer from being overprepossessing[2]. His rough clothes were old and slouchy[3]. The uppers of his shoes were too weak to carry the heavy re-soling[4] that was itself of no recent date. And his cotton shirt, a cheap, two shilling affair, showed a frayed[5] collar and ineradicable paint stains[6].

But it was Tom King's face that advertised him unmistakably for what he was. It was the face of a typical prizefighter[7]; of one who had put in long years of service in the squared ring and, by that means, developed and emphasized all the marks of the fighting beast. It was distinctly a lowering countenance[8], and, that no feature[9] of it might escape notice[10], it was clean-shaven[11]. The lips were shapeless and constituted a mouth harsh to excess, that was like a gash in his face. The jaw was aggressive, brutal, heavy. The eyes, slow of movement and heavy-lidded[12], were almost expressionless under the shaggy, indrawn brows[13]. Sheer animal that he was[14], the eyes were the most animal-like feature about him. They were sleepy, lion-like—the eyes of a fighting animal. The forehead slanted[15] quickly back to the hair, which, clipped close, showed every bump[16] of a villainous-looking head. A nose twice broken and moulded variously by countless blows[17], and a cauliflower ear, permanently swollen[18] and

---

1 **stolid-looking:** impassível • 2 **overprepossessing:** muito atraente • 3 **slouchy:** deformada • 4 **re-soling:** sola dupla • 5 **frayed:** gasto • 6 **stains:** manchas • 7 **prizefighter:** boxeador profissional • 8 **lowering countenance:** rosto sombrio • 9 **feature:** traço • 10 **escape notice:** passar inadvertido • 11 **clean-shaven:** bem barbeado • 12 **heavy-lidded:** com as pálpebras caídas • 13 **shaggy, indrawn brows:** sobrancelhas peludas e apontando para dentro • 14 **sheer animal that he was:** como o autêntico animal que era • 15 **slanted:** inclinada • 16 **bump:** calombo; protuberância • 17 **blows:** golpes • 18 **swollen:** inchada

distorted to twice its size, completed his adornment, while the beard, fresh-shaven as it was, sprouted[1] in the skin and gave the face a blue-black stain.

Altogether[2], it was the face of a man to be afraid of in a dark alley[3] or lonely place. And yet Tom King was not a criminal, nor had he ever done anything criminal. Outside of brawls[4], common to his walk in life[5], he had harmed no one. Nor had he ever been known to pick a quarrel[6]. He was a professional, and all the fighting brutishness of him was reserved for his professional appearances. Outside the ring he was slow-going, easy-natured, and, in his younger days, when money was flush[7], too open-handed for his own good. He bore no grudges[8] and had few enemies. Fighting was a business with him. In the ring he struck to hurt, struck to maim[9], struck to destroy; but there was no animus[10] in it. It was a plain business proposition. Audiences assembled and paid for the spectacle of men knocking each other out. The winner took the big end of the purse[11]. When Tom King faced the Woolloomoolloo Gouger, twenty years before, he knew that the Gouger's jaw was only four months healed[12] after having been broken in a Newcastle bout[13]. And he had played for that jaw and broken it again in the ninth round, not because he bore the Gouger any ill-will[14], but because that was the surest way to put the Gouger out[15] and win the

1 **sprouted:** brotava • 2 **altogether:** em geral • 3 **dark alley:** beco escuro • **outside of brawls:** longe de brigas • 5 **his walk in life:** seu estilo de vida • 6 **quarrel:** briga; rixa • 7 **when money was flush:** quando estava bem de dinheiro • 8 **he bore no grudges:** não guardava rancor de ninguém • 9 **maim:** destroçar • 10 **animus:** rancor; inimizade • 11 **purse:** carteira • 12 **was only four months healed:** fazia só quatro meses que estava curada • 13 **bout:** combate • 14 **he bore ... any ill-will:** lhe desejara algum mal • 15 **to put the Gouger out:** deixar Gouger sem sentido

big end of the purse. Nor had the Gouger borne him any ill-will for it. It was the game, and both knew the game and played it.

Tom King had never been a talker, and he sat by the window, morosely silent[1], staring at his hands. The veins stood out on the backs of the hands, large and swollen; and the knuckles[2], smashed and battered and malformed, testified to the use to which they had been put. He had never heard that a man's life was the life of his arteries, but well he knew the meaning of those big upstanding veins. His heart had pumped[3] too much blood through them at top pressure. They no longer did the work. He had stretched the elasticity out of them[4], and with their distension had passed his endurance[5]. He tired easily now. No longer could he do a fast twenty rounds, hammer and tongs[6], fight, fight, fight, from gong to gong, with fierce rally[7] on top of fierce rally, beaten to the ropes and in turn beating his opponent to the ropes, and rallying fiercest and fastest of all in that last, twentieth round, with the house[8] on its feet and yelling, himself rushing[9], striking[10], ducking[11], raining showers of blows[12] upon showers of blows and receiving showers of blows in return, and all the time the heart faithfully[13] pumping the surging blood[14] through the adequate veins. The veins, swollen at the time, had always shrunk down[15] again, though

---

1 **morosely silent:** num silêncio taciturno • 2 **knuckles:** articulações dos dedos • 3 **had pumped:** havia bombeado • 4 **he had stretched the elasticity out of them:** haviam perdido sua elasticidade (as veias) • 5 **endurance:** resistência • 6 **hammer and tongs:** aos apertos • 7 **rally:** ofensiva • 8 **the house:** o público • 9 **rushing:** atacando • 10 **striking:** batendo • 11 **ducking:** agachando-se • 12 **raining showers of blows:** acertando uma chuva de golpes • 13 **faithfully:** religiosamente • 14 **surging blood:** sangue acelerado • 15 **shrunk down:** contraído

each time, imperceptibly at first, not quite—remaining just a trifle[1] larger than before. He stared at them and at his battered knuckles, and, for the moment, caught a vision of the youthful excellence of those hands before the first knuckle had been smashed on the head of Benny Jones, otherwise known as the Welsh[2] Terror.

The impression of his hunger came back on him.

"Blimey, but couldn't I go a piece of steak[3]!" he muttered aloud, clenching his huge fists[4] and spitting out a smothered oath[5].

"I tried both Burke's an' Sawley's," his wife said half apologetically[6].

"An' they wouldn't?" he demanded.

"Not a ha'penny. Burke said—" She faltered[7].

"G'wan[8]! Wot'd he say[9]?"

"As how 'e was thinkin' Sandel ud do ye[10] to-night, an' as how yer score[11] was comfortable big as it was."

Tom King grunted, but did not reply. He was busy thinking of the bull terrier he had kept in his younger days to which he had fed steaks without end. Burke would have given him credit for a thousand steaks—then. But times had changed. Tom King was getting old; and old men, fighting before second-rate clubs, couldn't expect to run bills[12] of any size with the tradesmen[13].

---

1 **a trifle:** um pouquinho • 2 **Welsh:** galês • 3 **blimey, but couldn't I go a piece of steak:** caramba, eu comeria um bife... • 4 **clenching his huge fists:** cerrando os punhos enormes • 5 **spitting out a smothered oath:** cuspindo um juramento sufocado • 6 **half apologetically:** meio desculpando-se • 7 **she faltered:** balbuciou • 8 **g'wan! (go on!):** adiante! • 9 **wot'd he say? (what did he say?):** o que ele disse? • 10 **ud do ye (would do you):** lhe machucaria • 11 **yer score (your score):** sua pontuação • 12 **to run bills:** ter dívidas • 13 **tradesmen:** comerciantes

He had got up in the morning with a longing for[1] a piece of steak, and the longing had not abated[2]. He had not had a fair training for this fight. It was a drought year[3] in Australia, times were hard, and even the most irregular work was difficult to find. He had had no sparring partner, and his food had not been of the best nor always sufficient. He had done a few days' navvy[4] work when he could get it, and he had run around the Domain[5] in the early mornings to get his legs in shape. But it was hard, training without a partner and with a wife and two kiddies that must be fed[6]. Credit with the tradesmen had undergone very slight expansion[7] when he was matched[8] with Sandel. The secretary of the Gayety Club had advanced him three pounds—the loser's end of the purse—and beyond that had refused to go. Now and again[9] he had managed to borrow a few shillings from old pals[10], who would have lent[11] more only that it was a drought year and they were hard put[12] themselves. No—and there was no use in disguising[13] the fact—his training had not been satisfactory. He should have had better food and no worries. Besides, when a man is forty, it is harder to get into condition[14] than when he is twenty.

"What time is it, Lizzie?" he asked.

His wife went across the hall to inquire, and came back.

"Quarter before eight."

---

1 **a longing for:** desejando • 2 **had not abated:** não havia diminuído • 3 **a drought year:** um ano de seca • 4 **navvy:** trabalhador braçal • 5 **the Domain:** parque de Sydney • 6 **that must be fed:** que tinha que alimentar • 7 **credit ... had undergone very slight expansion:** não ampliaram muito seu crédito • 8 **he was matched:** estava equiparado com • 9 **now and again:** de vez em quando • 10 **old pals:** velhos colegas • 11 **would have lent:** emprestariam • 12 **they were hard put:** estavam passando por dificuldades financeiras; estavam num aperto • 13 **disguising:** ocultar • 14 **to get into condition:** entrar em forma

"They'll be startin' the first bout in a few minutes," he said. "Only a try-out[1]. Then there's a four-round spar[2] 'tween[3] Dealer Wells an' Gridley, an' a ten-round go 'tween Starlight an' some sailor bloke[4]. I don't come on for over an hour."

At the end of another silent ten minutes, he rose to his feet.

"Truth is, Lizzie, I ain't had proper trainin'."

He reached for his hat and started for the door. He did not offer to kiss her—he never did on going out—but on this night she dared[5] to kiss him, throwing her arms around him and compelling him to bend down[6] to her face. She looked quite small against the massive bulk[7] of the man.

"Good luck, Tom," she said. "You gotter do 'im[8]."

"Ay[9], I gotter do 'im," he repeated. "That's all there is to it[10]. I jus' gotter do 'im."

He laughed with an attempt at heartiness[11], while she pressed more closely against him. Across her shoulders he looked around the bare room[12]. It was all he had in the world, with the rent overdue[13], and her and the kiddies. And he was leaving it to go out into the night to get meat for his mate and cubs[14]—not like a modern working-man going to his machine grind[15], but in the old, primitive, royal, animal way, by fighting for it.

1 **try-out:** prova • 2 **spar:** treinamento • 3 **'tween (between):** entre • 4 **some sailor bloke:** um marinheiro (bloke significa "cara", "sujeito") • 5 **she dared:** atreveu-se • 6 **compelling him to bend down:** obrigando-o a agachar-se • 7 **the massive bulk:** o enorme corpo • 8 **you gotter do 'im (you have to do him):** você tem de dar uma surra nele • 9 **ay:** sim (forma oral) • 10 **that's all there is to it:** isso é tudo • 11 **with an attempt at heartiness:** tentando parecer sincero • 12 **bare room:** sala nua; cômodo com poucos móveis • 13 **the rent overdue:** aluguel atrasado • 14 **for his mate and cubs:** para sua companheira e seus filhinhos • 15 **machine grind:** máquina de moer

"I gotter do 'im," he repeated, this time a hint[1] of desperation in his voice. "If it's a win, it's thirty quid[2]—an' I can pay all that's owin', with a lump o' money left over[3]. If it's a lose, I get naught[4]—not even a penny for me to ride home on the tram[5]. The secretary's give all that's comin' from a loser's end. Good-bye, old woman. I'll come straight home if it's a win."

"An' I'll be waitin' up[6]," she called to him along the hall.

It was full two miles to the Gayety, and as he walked along he remembered how in his palmy days[7]—he had once been the heavyweight champion of New South Wales[8]—he would have ridden in a cab[9] to the fight, and how, most likely[10], some heavy backer[11] would have paid for the cab and ridden with him. There were Tommy Burns and that Yankee nigger[12], Jack Johnson—they rode about in motor-cars. And he walked! And, as any man knew, a hard two miles was not the best preliminary to a fight. He was an old un[13], and the world did not wag well[14] with old uns. He was good for nothing now except navvy work, and his broken nose and swollen ear were against him even in that. He found himself wishing that he had learned a trade[15]. It would have been better in the long run[16]. But no one had told him, and he knew, deep down in his heart, that he would not have

---

1 **hint:** rastro • 2 **thirty quid:** trinta libras (australianas) • 3 **with a lump o' money left over:** com uma sobra de dinheiro; com um dinheirinho a mais • 4 **I get naught:** não ganho nada • 5 **tram:** bonde • 6 **an' I'll be waitin' up (and I'll be waiting up):** vou lhe esperar acordada • 7 **palmy days:** dias de glória • 8 **New South Wales:** Nova Gales do Sul (Estado do sudeste da Austrália) • 9 **cab:** táxi • 10 **most likely:** com certeza • 11 **backer:** fã; aficionado • 12 **nigger:** negro • 13 **old un:** um velho • 14 **did not wag well:** não se dava bem • 15 **trade:** ocupação; ofício • 16 **in the long run:** a longo prazo

listened if they had. It had been so easy. Big money—sharp[1], glorious fights—periods of rest and loafing[2] in between—a following of eager flatterers[3], the slaps on the back[4], the shakes of the hand, the toffs[5] glad to buy him a drink for the privilege of five minutes' talk—and the glory of it, the yelling houses, the whirlwind finish[6], the referee's "King wins!" and his name in the sporting columns next day.

Those had been times! But he realized now, in his slow, ruminating[7] way, that it was the old uns he had been putting away[8]. He was Youth, rising; and they were Age, sinking[9]. No wonder it had been easy—they with their swollen veins and battered[10] knuckles and weary[11] in the bones of them from the long battles they had already fought. He remembered the time he put out old Stowsher Bill, at Rush-Cutters Bay, in the eighteenth round, and how old Bill had cried afterward in the dressing-room like a baby. Perhaps old Bill's rent had been overdue. Perhaps he'd had at home a missus[12] an' a couple of kiddies. And perhaps Bill, that very day of the fight, had had a hungering for a piece of steak. Bill had fought game and taken incredible punishment. He could see now, after he had gone through the mill[13] himself, that Stowsher Bill had fought for a bigger stake[14], that night twenty years ago, than had young Tom King, who had

---

1 **sharp:** intensas • 2 **loafing:** descanso • 3 **eager flatterers:** aduladores entusiastas • 4 **the slaps on the back:** os tapinhas nas costas • 5 **toffs:** exibidos • 6 **whirlwind finish:** a voragem do final • 7 **ruminating:** reflexivo • 8 **he had been putting away:** havia deixado de lado • 9 **sinking:** afogando-se • 10 **battered:** espancado • 11 **weary:** cansado • 12 **missus:** patroa; senhora; mulher • 13 **after he had gone through the mill:** depois de ter passado por isso • 14 **had fought for a bigger stake:** havia lutado por algo mais importante

fought for glory and easy money. No wonder Stowsher Bill had cried afterward in the dressing-room.

Well, a man had only so many fights in him, to begin with. It was the iron law of the game. One man might have a hundred hard fights in him, another man only twenty; each, according to the make of him[1] and the quality of his fibre, had a definite number, and, when he had fought them, he was done. Yes, he had had more fights in him than most of them, and he had had far more than his share of the hard, gruelling fights[2]—the kind that worked the heart and lungs to bursting[3], that took the elastic out of the arteries and made hard knots of muscle out of Youth's sleek suppleness[4], that wore out[5] nerve and stamina and made brain and bones weary from excess of effort and endurance overwrought[6]. Yes, he had done better than all of them. There were none of his old fighting partners left. He was the last of the old guard. He had seen them all finished, and he had had a hand in[7] finishing some of them.

They had tried him out[8] against the old uns, and one after another he had put them away—laughing when, like old Stowsher Bill, they cried in the dressing-room. And now he was an old un, and they tried out the youngsters on him. There was that bloke, Sandel. He had come over from New Zealand with a record behind him. But nobody in Australia knew anything about him, so they put him up against old

---

1 **the make of him:** sua forma de ser • 2 **he had had far more than his share of hard, gruelling fights:** havia superado há muito tempo sua parte de combates duros e extenuantes • 3 **worked ... to bursting:** arrebentava • 4 **sleek suppleness:** elegante agilidade • 5 **wore out:** desgastavam • 6 **effort and endurance overwrought:** excesso de esforço e resistência • 7 **he had had a hand in:** havia tomado parte em; havia participado de • 8 **they had tried him out:** o haviam testado

Tom King. If Sandel made a showing¹, he would be given better men to fight, with bigger purses to win; so it was to be depended upon that he would put up a fierce battle². He had everything to win by it—money and glory and career; and Tom King was the grizzled³ old chopping-block⁴ that guarded⁵ the highway to fame and fortune. And he had nothing to win except thirty quid, to pay to the landlord and the tradesmen. And, as Tom King thus ruminated, there came to his stolid vision the form of Youth, glorious Youth, rising exultant and invincible, supple of muscle⁶ and silken of skin⁷, with heart and lungs that had never been tired and torn and that laughed at limitation of effort. Yes, Youth was the Nemesis. It destroyed the old uns and recked not that⁸, in so doing, it destroyed itself. It enlarged its arteries and smashed its knuckles, and was in turn destroyed by Youth. For Youth was ever youthful. It was only Age that grew old.

At Castlereagh Street he turned to the left, and three blocks along came to the Gayety. A crowd of young larrikins⁹ hanging outside the door made respectful way for him, and he heard one say to another: "That's 'im! That's Tom King!"

Inside, on the way to his dressing-room, he encountered the secretary, a keen-eyed¹⁰, shrewd-faced¹¹ young man, who shook his hand.

"How are you feelin', Tom?" he asked.

---

1 **showing:** boa atuação • 2 **he would put up a fierce battle:** apresentaria uma dura batalha • 3 **grizzled:** grisalho • 4 **chopping-block:** tábua de cortar • 5 **guarded:** protegia • 6 **supple of muscle:** de músculos ágeis • 7 **silken of skin:** de pele sedosa • 8 **recked not that:** não percebia que • 9 **larrikins:** arruaceiros • 10 **keen-eyed:** de olhos abertos • 11 **shrewd-faced:** de fisionomia astuta

"Fit as a fiddle[1]," King answered, though he knew that he lied, and that if he had a quid, he would give it right there for a good piece of steak.

When he emerged from the dressing-room, his seconds[2] behind him, and came down the aisle[3] to the squared ring in the centre of the hall, a burst[4] of greeting and applause went up from the waiting crowd. He acknowledged[5] salutations right and left, though few of the faces did he know. Most of them were the faces of kiddies unborn[6] when he was winning his first laurels in the squared ring. He leaped[7] lightly to the raised platform and ducked through the ropes to his corner, where he sat down on a folding stool[8]. Jack Ball, the referee, came over and shook his hand. Ball was a broken-down[9] pugilist who for over ten years had not entered the ring as a principal. King was glad that he had him for referee. They were both old uns. If he should rough it with Sandel a bit beyond the rules[10], he knew Ball could be depended upon to pass it by.

Aspiring young heavyweights, one after another, were climbing into the ring and being presented to the audience by the referee. Also, he issued their challenges[11] for them.

"Young Pronto," Bill announced, "from North Sydney, challenges the winner for fifty pounds side bet[12]."

The audience applauded, and applauded again as Sandel

---

1 **fit as a fiddle:** forte como um touro • 2 **seconds:** segundos (assistentes do pugilista) • 3 **aisle:** corredor • 4 **burst:** estouro • 5 **he acknowledged:** respondeu • 6 **kiddies unborn:** garotos que ainda não haviam nascido • 7 **he leaped:** saltou • 8 **folding stool:** tamborete dobrável • 9 **broken-down:** acabado • 10 **if he should rough it ... a bit beyond the rules:** se tivesse de levar a regra ao limite • 11 **he issued their challenges:** ele anunciou seus desafios • 12 **side bet:** aposta complementar

himself sprang¹ through the ropes and sat down in his corner. Tom King looked across the ring at him curiously, for in a few minutes they would be locked together in merciless² combat, each trying with all the force of him to knock the other into unconsciousness. But little could he see, for Sandel, like himself, had trousers and sweater on over his ring costume. His face was strongly handsome, crowned with a curly mop of yellow hair³, while his thick, muscular neck hinted at bodily magnificence⁴.

Young Pronto went to one corner and then the other, shaking hands with the principals and dropping down out of the ring. The challenges went on. Ever Youth climbed through the ropes—Youth unknown, but insatiable—crying out to mankind⁵ that with strength and skill it would match issues with the winner. A few years before, in his own heyday⁶ of invincibleness, Tom King would have been amused⁷ and bored by these preliminaries. But now he sat fascinated, unable to shake the vision of Youth from his eyes. Always were these youngsters rising up in the boxing game, springing through the ropes and shouting their defiance⁸; and always were the old uns going down⁹ before them. They climbed to success over the bodies of the old uns. And ever they came, more and more youngsters—Youth unquenchable¹⁰ and irresistible—and ever they put the old uns away, themselves becoming old uns and travelling the same downward path, while behind them, ever pressing on them, was

1 **sprang:** saltou • 2 **merciless:** sem piedade • 3 **crowned with a curly mop of yellow hair:** coroado com um chumaço de cabelo louro encaracolado • 4 **hinted at bodily magnificence:** insinuava um esplendor físico • 5 **mankind:** a humanidade • 6 **heyday:** apogeu • 7 **would have been amused:** teria se divertido • 8 **defiance:** rebeldia • 9 **going down:** caindo • 10 **unquenchable:** insaciável

Youth eternal—the new babies, grown lusty[1] and dragging their elders[2] down, with behind them more babies to the end of time—Youth that must have its will[3] and that will never die.

King glanced over to the press box[4] and nodded to Morgan, of *The Sportsman*, and Corbett, of *The Referee*[5]. Then he held out his hands, while Sid Sullivan and Charley Bates, his seconds, slipped on his gloves and laced them tight[6], closely watched by one of Sandel's seconds, who first examined critically the tapes on King's knuckles. A second of his own was in Sandel's corner, performing a like office[7]. Sandel's trousers were pulled off, and, as he stood up, his sweater was skinned off[8] over his head. And Tom King, looking, saw Youth incarnate, deep-chested[9], heavy-thewed[10], with muscles that slipped and slid[11] like live things under the white satin skin. The whole body was a crawl with life[12], and Tom King knew that it was a life that had never oozed[13] its freshness out through the aching pores during the long fights wherein[14] Youth paid its toll[15] and departed not quite so young as when it entered.

The two men advanced to meet each other, and, as the gong sounded and the seconds clattered out of the ring[16] with the folding stools, they shook hands and instantly took their

---

1 **lusty:** robustos • 2 **elders:** mais velhos • 3 **will:** vontade • 4 **press box:** tribuna de imprensa • 5 **The Sportsman, The Referee:** publicações desportivas da época • 6 **laced them tight:** os ataram com força • 7 **performing a like office:** fazendo o mesmo • 8 **his sweater was skinned off:** tiraram seu abrigo • 9 **deep-chested:** de peito largo • 10 **heavy-thewed:** de músculos fortes • 11 **slipped and slid:** deslizavam • 12 **was a crawl with life:** transparecia vitalidade • 13 **oozed:** gotejado • 14 **wherein:** em que • 15 **paid its toll:** pagava um preço alto • 16 **clattered out of the ring:** pularam do ringue

fighting attitudes. And instantly, like a mechanism of steel and springs[1] balanced on a hair trigger[2], Sandel was in and out and in again, landing a left to the eyes, a right to the ribs, ducking a counter, dancing lightly away and dancing menacingly back again. He was swift[3] and clever. It was a dazzling[4] exhibition. The house yelled its approbation. But King was not dazzled. He had fought too many fights and too many youngsters. He knew the blows for what they were—too quick and too deft[5] to be dangerous. Evidently Sandel was going to rush things[6] from the start. It was to be expected. It was the way of Youth, expending its splendour and excellence in wild insurgence and furious onslaught[7], overwhelming opposition with its own unlimited glory of strength and desire.

Sandel was in and out, here, there, and everywhere, light-footed and eager-hearted, a living wonder of white flesh and stinging[8] muscle that wove itself into a dazzling fabric[9] of attack, slipping and leaping like a flying shuttle[10] from action to action through a thousand actions, all of them centred upon the destruction of Tom King, who stood between him and fortune. And Tom King patiently endured[11]. He knew his business, and he knew Youth now that Youth was no longer his. There was nothing to do till the other lost some of his steam[12], was his thought, and he grinned to himself as he deliberately ducked so as to receive a heavy blow on

---

1 **steel and springs:** aço e molas • 2 **balanced on a hair trigger:** se desequilibra com um nada • 3 **swift:** rápido • 4 **dazzling:** deslumbrante • 5 **deft:** hábil • 6 **to rush things:** precipitar os acontecimentos • 7 **onslaught:** ataque • 8 **stinging:** contundentes • 9 **wove itself into a dazzling fabric:** se envolvia num tecido deslumbrante • 10 **flying shuttle:** lançadeira voadora • 11 **endured:** aguentou • 12 **steam:** energia

the top of his head. It was a wicked¹ thing to do, yet eminently fair according to the rules of the boxing game. A man was supposed to take care of his own knuckles, and, if he insisted on hitting an opponent on the top of the head, he did so at his own peril². King could have ducked lower and let the blow whiz³ harmlessly past, but he remembered his own early fights and how he smashed his first knuckle on the head of the Welsh Terror. He was but⁴ playing the game. That duck had accounted for⁵ one of Sandel's knuckles. Not that Sandel would mind it now⁶. He would go on, superbly regardless⁷, hitting as hard as ever throughout the fight. But later on, when the long ring battles had begun to tell, he would regret⁸ that knuckle and look back and remember how he smashed it on Tom King's head.

The first round was all Sandel's, and he had the house yelling with the rapidity of his whirlwind rushes⁹. He overwhelmed¹⁰ King with avalanches of punches, and King did nothing. He never struck once, contenting himself with covering up, blocking and ducking and clinching¹¹ to avoid punishment. He occasionally feinted¹², shook his head when the weight of a punch landed, and moved stolidly about, never leaping or springing¹³ or wasting an ounce of strength. Sandel must foam the froth of Youth away¹⁴ before discreet Age could dare to retaliate¹⁵. All King's movements were slow

1 **wicked:** mal-intencionada • 2 **at his own peril:** por sua conta e risco • 3 **whiz:** passara a toda velocidade • 4 **he was but:** só estava • 5 **had accounted for:** havia esmagado • 6 **not that ... would mind it now:** não o causaria agora • 7 **superbly regardless:** soberbamente despreocupado • 8 **he would regret:** lamentaria • 9 **rushes:** ataques • 10 **he overwhelmed:** ele sobrepujou • 11 **clinching:** abraçando-se • 12 **feinted:** fintava • 13 **never leaping or springing:** sem saltar nem bailar • 14 **must foam the froth ... away:** devia eliminar a vitalidade • 15 **to retaliate:** retaliar; contra-atacar

and methodical, and his heavy-lidded, slow-moving eyes gave him the appearance of being half asleep or dazed[1]. Yet they were eyes that saw everything, that had been trained to see everything through all his twenty years and odd[2] in the ring. They were eyes that did not blink[3] or waver[4] before an impending[5] blow, but that coolly[6] saw and measured distance.

Seated in his corner for the minute's rest at the end of the round, he lay back with outstretched legs[7], his arms resting on the right angle of the ropes, his chest and abdomen heaving[8] frankly and deeply as he gulped down[9] the air driven by the towels of his seconds. He listened with closed eyes to the voices of the house, "Why don't yeh[10] fight, Tom?" many were crying. "Yeh ain't afraid of 'im, are yeh[11]?"

"Muscle-bound[12]," he heard a man on a front seat comment. "He can't move quicker. Two to one on Sandel, in quids."

The gong struck and the two men advanced from their corners. Sandel came forward fully three-quarters of the distance, eager to begin again; but King was content to[13] advance the shorter distance. It was in line with his policy of economy. He had not been well trained, and he had not had enough to eat, and every step counted. Besides, he had already walked two miles to the ringside. It was a repetition of

---

1 **dazed:** aturdido • 2 **twenty years and odd:** vinte e tantos anos • 3 **blink:** piscar • 4 **waver:** vacilavam • 5 **impending:** iminente • 6 **coolly:** com serenidade • 7 **outstretched legs:** pernas esticadas • 8 **heaving:** respirando • 9 **gulped down:** engolia • 10 **yeh (you):** você • 11 **yeh ain't afraid of 'im, are yeh? (you are not afraid of him, are you?):** você não está com medo dele, está? • 12 **muscle-bound:** músculos rígidos • 13 **was content to:** se contentava em

the first round, with Sandel attacking like a whirlwind and with the audience indignantly demanding[1] why King did not fight. Beyond feinting and several slowly delivered and ineffectual blows he did nothing save block and stall[2] and clinch. Sandel wanted to make the pace[3] fast, while King, out of his wisdom, refused to accommodate him[4]. He grinned with a certain wistful pathos[5] in his ring-battered countenance, and went on cherishing[6] his strength with the jealousy of which only Age is capable. Sandel was Youth, and he threw his strength away with the munificent[7] abandon of Youth. To King belonged the ring generalship[8], the wisdom bred[9] of long, aching fights. He watched with cool eyes and head, moving slowly and waiting for Sandel's froth to foam away. To the majority of the onlookers[10] it seemed as though King was hopelessly outclassed[11], and they voiced their opinion in offers of three to one on Sandel. But there were wise ones, a few, who knew King of old time, and who covered what they considered easy money.

The third round began as usual, one-sided, with Sandel doing all the leading[12], and delivering all the punishment. A half-minute had passed when Sandel, over-confident, left an opening. King's eyes and right arm flashed in the same instant. It was his first real blow—a hook[13], with the twisted arch of the arm to make it rigid, and with all the weight of

---

1 **demanding:** perguntando-se • 2 **save block and stall:** exceto bloquear e esquivar-se • 3 **pace:** ritmo • 4 **accommodate him:** agradar • 5 **wistful pathos:** *páthos* melancólico • 6 **cherishing:** conservando • 7 **munificient:** generoso • 8 **generalship:** generalato (posto de general) • 9 **bred:** nascida • 10 **onlookers:** espectadores • 11 **outclassed:** superado • 12 **doing all the leading:** dominando • 13 **a hook:** um gancho

the half-pivoted[1] body behind it. It was like a sleepy-seeming lion suddenly thrusting out a lightning paw[2]. Sandel, caught on the side of the jaw[3], was felled[4] like a bullock[5]. The audience gasped and murmured awe-stricken[6] applause. The man was not muscle-bound, after all, and he could drive a blow like a trip-hammer[7].

Sandel was shaken[8]. He rolled over and attempted to rise, but the sharp yells from his seconds to take the count[9] restrained him[10]. He knelt on one knee, ready to rise, and waited, while the referee stood over him, counting the seconds loudly in his ear. At the ninth he rose in fighting attitude, and Tom King, facing him, knew regret that the blow had not been an inch nearer the point of the jaw. That would have been a knock-out[11], and he could have carried the thirty quid home to the missus and the kiddies.

The round continued to the end of its three minutes, Sandel for the first time respectful of his opponent and King slow of movement and sleepy-eyed as ever[12]. As the round neared its close, King, warned of the fact by sight of[13] the seconds crouching[14] outside ready for the spring in through the ropes, worked the fight around to his own corner. And when the gong struck, he sat down immediately on the waiting stool, while Sandel had to walk all the way across the diagonal of the square to his own corner. It was a little thing,

---

1 **half-pivoted:** em meio giro • 2 **thrusting out a lightning paw:** que dá uma patada com a velocidade de um raio • 3 **jaw:** mandíbula • 4 **was felled:** caiu derrubado • 5 **bullock:** boi • 6 **awe-stricken:** improvisado • 7 **trip-hammer:** martelo a vapor • 8 **shaken:** abalado • 9 **to take the count:** esperara a contagem • 10 **restrained him:** o contiveram • 11 **knock-out:** nocaute • 12 **as ever:** como sempre • 13 **warned of the fact by sight of:** consciente disso ao ver • 14 **crouching:** contraídos

but it was the sum of little things that counted. Sandel was compelled[1] to walk that many more steps, to give up[2] that much energy, and to lose a part of the precious minute of rest. At the beginning of every round King loafed slowly out from his corner, forcing his opponent to advance the greater distance. The end of every round found the fight manoeuvred by King into his own corner so that he could immediately sit down.

Two more rounds went by[3], in which King was parsimonious of effort and Sandel prodigal[4]. The latter's attempt[5] to force a fast pace made King uncomfortable, for a fair percentage of the multitudinous blows showered upon him[6] went home[7]. Yet King persisted in his dogged[8] slowness, despite the crying of the young hot-heads[9] for him to go in and fight. Again, in the sixth round, Sandel was careless[10], again Tom King's fearful[11] right flashed out[12] to the jaw, and again Sandel took the nine seconds count.

By the seventh round Sandel's pink of condition[13] was gone, and he settled down[14] to what he knew was to be the hardest fight in his experience. Tom King was an old un, but a better old un than he had ever encountered—an old un who never lost his head, who was remarkably able at defence, whose blows had the impact of a knotted club, and who had a knockout in either hand. Nevertheless, Tom King dared

---

1 **was compelled:** se viu obrigado a • 2 **to give up:** investir • 3 **went by:** transcorreram • 4 **prodigal:** pródigo; esbanjador • 5 **the latter's attempt:** a intenção deste último • 6 **showered upon him:** que choveram sobre ele • 7 **went home:** deram em nada • 8 **dogged slowness:** lentidão obstinada • 9 **hot-heads:** exaltados • 10 **careless:** descuidado • 11 **fearful:** atemorizante • 12 **flashed out:** saiu disparado • 13 **pink of condition:** excelente forma física • 14 **he settled down:** se preparou

not hit often. He never forgot his battered knuckles, and knew that every hit must count if the knuckles were to last out¹ the fight. As he sat in his corner, glancing across at his opponent, the thought came to him that the sum of his wisdom and Sandel's youth would constitute a world's champion heavyweight. But that was the trouble. Sandel would never become a world champion. He lacked² the wisdom, and the only way for him to get it was to buy it with Youth; and when wisdom was his, Youth would have been spent³ in buying it.

King took every advantage he knew. He never missed⁴ an opportunity to clinch, and in effecting most of the clinches his shoulder drove stiffly into the other's ribs⁵. In the philosophy of the ring a shoulder was as good as a punch so far as damage was concerned⁶, and a great deal better⁷ so far as concerned expenditure of effort⁸. Also, in the clinches King rested his weight on his opponent, and was loath to let go⁹. This compelled the interference of the referee, who tore them apart¹⁰, always assisted by Sandel, who had not yet learned to rest. He could not refrain from¹¹ using those glorious flying arms and writhing¹² muscles of his, and when the other rushed into a clinch, striking shoulder against ribs, and with head resting under Sandel's left arm, Sandel almost

---

1 **if the knuckles were to last out:** se queria que as articulações resistissem • 2 **he lacked:** carecia de; precisava de • 3 **Youth would have been spent:** teria gasto sua juventude • 4 **missed:** deixava escapar • 5 **his shoulder drove stiffly into the other's ribs:** seu ombro forçava as costelas do rival • 6 **so far as ... concerned:** no que diz respeito a • 7 **a great deal better:** muitíssimo melhor • 8 **expenditure of effort:** despender esforços • 9 **was loath to let go:** resistia a soltá-lo • 10 **who tore them apart:** que os separou • 11 **refrain from:** absteve-se de • 12 **writhing:** retorcidos

invariably swung his right behind his own back and into the projecting face. It was a clever stroke, much admired by the audience, but it was not dangerous, and was, therefore[1], just that much wasted strength. But Sandel was tireless[2] and unaware[3] of limitations, and King grinned and doggedly endured.

Sandel developed a fierce right to the body, which made it appear that King was taking an enormous amount of punishment, and it was only the old ringsters[4] who appreciated the deft touch[5] of King's left glove to the other's biceps just before the impact of the blow. It was true, the blow landed each time; but each time it was robbed of its power by that touch on the biceps. In the ninth round, three times inside a minute, King's right hooked its twisted arch[6] to the jaw; and three times Sandel's body, heavy as it was, was levelled to the mat[7]. Each time he took the nine seconds allowed him and rose to his feet, shaken and jarred[8], but still strong. He had lost much of his speed, and he wasted less effort. He was fighting grimly[9]; but he continued to draw upon[10] his chief asset[11], which was Youth. King's chief asset was experience. As his vitality had dimmed[12] and his vigour abated, he had replaced them with cunning[13], with wisdom born of the long fights and with a careful shepherding of strength[14]. Not alone had he learned never to make a superfluous movement, but

---

1 **therefore:** portanto • 2 **tireless:** incansável • 3 **unaware:** sem perceber; sem se dar conta • 4 **ringsters:** fãs de boxe; aficionados • 5 **deft touch:** toque hábil • 6 **King's right hooked its twisted arch:** o gancho de direita de King golpeou • 7 **was levelled to the mat:** acabou beijando a lona • 8 **jarred:** chocado • 9 **grimly:** com todas as forças • 10 **draw upon:** recorrendo • 11 **chief asset:** principal assistente • 12 **had dimmed:** se apagara • 13 **cunning:** astúcia • 14 **with a careful shepherding of strength:** administrando cuidadosamente as forças

he had learned how to seduce an opponent into throwing his strength away. Again and again, by feint of foot and hand and body he continued to inveigle[1] Sandel into leaping back, ducking, or countering[2]. King rested, but he never permitted Sandel to rest. It was the strategy of Age.

Early in the tenth round King began stopping the other's rushes with straight lefts to the face, and Sandel, grown wary[3], responded by drawing the left, then by ducking it and delivering his right in a swinging hook to the side of the head. It was too high up to be vitally effective; but when first it landed, King knew the old, familiar descent of the black veil[4] of unconsciousness[5] across his mind. For the instant, or for the slighest fraction of an instant, rather, he ceased. In the one moment he saw his opponent ducking out of his field of vision and the background[6] of white, watching faces; in the next moment he again saw his opponent and the background of faces. It was as if he had slept for a time and just opened his eyes again, and yet the interval of unconsciousness was so microscopically short that there had been no time for him to fall. The audience saw him totter[7] and his knees give[8], and then saw him recover and tuck[9] his chin deeper into the shelter[10] of his left shoulder.

Several times Sandel repeated the blow, keeping King partially dazed, and then the latter worked out his defence, which was also a counter. Feinting with his left he took a half-step backward, at the same time upper cutting with the

---

1 **inveigle:** adulando • 2 **countering:** reagira • 3 **grown wary:** mais cauteloso • 4 **veil:** véu • 5 **unconsciousness:** inconsciência • 6 **background:** fundo • 7 **totter:** cambalear • 8 **give:** ceder • 9 **tuck:** enfiou • 10 **shelter:** refúgio

whole strength of his right. So accurately was it timed[1] that it landed squarely[2] on Sandel's face in the full, downward sweep of the duck[3], and Sandel lifted in the air and curled backward, striking the mat on his head and shoulders. Twice King achieved this, then turned loose[4] and hammered[5] his opponent to the ropes. He gave Sandel no chance to rest or to set himself, but smashed blow in upon blow till the house rose to its feet and the air was filled with an unbroken roar[6] of applause. But Sandel's strength and endurance were superb, and he continued to stay on his feet. A knock-out seemed certain, and a captain of police, appalled at the dreadful punishment[7], arose by the ringside to stop the fight. The gong struck for the end of the round and Sandel staggered[8] to his corner, protesting to the captain that he was sound[9] and strong. To prove it, he threw two back-air-springs[10], and the police captain gave in[11].

Tom King, leaning back[12] in his corner and breathing hard[13], was disappointed. If the fight had been stopped, the referee, perforce[14], would have rendered him the decision[15] and the purse would have been his. Unlike Sandel, he was not fighting for glory or career, but for thirty quid. And now Sandel would recuperate in the minute of rest.

Youth will be served[16]—this saying[17] flashed into King's

---

1 **so accurately was it timed:** sincronizou-o com tanta precisão • 2 **squarely:** diretamente • 3 **downward sweep of the duck:** quando se agachava para esquivar-se • 4 **turned loose:** se soltou • 5 **hammered:** espancou • 6 **unbroken roar:** rugido ininterrupto • 7 **dreadful punishment:** castigo atroz • 8 **staggered:** cambaleou • 9 **sound:** bem • 10 **back-air-springs:** saltos para trás • 11 **gave in:** cedeu • 12 **leaning back:** recostado • 13 **breathing hard:** respirando com dificuldade • 14 **perforce:** por obrigação • 15 **would have rendered him the decision:** lhe daria a vitória por pontos • 16 **Youth will be served:** a juventude triunfaria • 17 **saying:** dito

mind, and he remembered the first time he had heard it, the night when he had put away¹ Stowsher Bill. The toff who had bought him a drink after the fight and patted him² on the shoulder had used those words. Youth will be served! The toff was right. And on that night in the long ago³ he had been Youth. To-night Youth sat in the opposite corner. As for himself⁴, he had been fighting for half an hour now, and he was an old man. Had he fought like Sandel, he would not have lasted fifteen minutes. But the point was that he did not recuperate. Those upstanding arteries and that sorely tired⁵ heart would not enable him to gather strength⁶ in the intervals between the rounds. And he had not had sufficient strength in him to begin with. His legs were heavy under him⁷ and beginning to cramp⁸. He should not have walked those two miles to the fight. And there was the steak which he had got up longing for that morning. A great and terrible hatred⁹ rose up in him for the butchers¹⁰ who had refused him credit. It was hard for an old man to go into a fight without enough to eat. And a piece of steak was such a little thing, a few pennies at best; yet it meant thirty quid to him.

With the gong that opened the eleventh round, Sandel rushed, making a show of freshness which he did not really possess. King knew it for what it was—a bluff¹¹ as old as the game itself. He clinched to save himself, then, going free, allowed Sandel to get set¹². This was what King desired. He

---

1 **he had put away:** havia derrotado • 2 **patted him:** havia dado uns tapinhas • 3 **in the long ago:** muito tempo atrás • 4 **as for himself:** quanto a ele • 5 **sorely tired:** muito cansado • 6 **to gather strenght:** reunir forças • 7 **his legs were heavy under him:** suas pernas pesavam • 8 **to cramp:** ter câimbras • 9 **hatred:** ódio • 10 **butchers:** açougueiros • 11 **bluff:** blefe • 12 **to get set:** preparar-se

feinted with his left, drew the answering duck and swinging upward hook, then made the half-step backward, delivered the upper cut[1] full to the face and crumpled[2] Sandel over to the mat. After that he never let him rest, receiving punishment himself, but inflicting far more, smashing Sandel to the ropes, hooking and driving all manner of blows into him, tearing away from his clinches or punching him out of attempted clinches, and ever when Sandel would have fallen, catching him with one uplifting hand and with the other immediately smashing him into the ropes where he could not fall.

The house by this time had gone mad[3], and it was his house, nearly every voice yelling: "Go it, Tom!" "Get 'im! Get 'im!" "You've got 'im, Tom! You've got 'im!" It was to be[4] a whirlwind finish, and that was what a ringside audience paid to see.

And Tom King, who for half an hour had conserved his strength, now expended[5] it prodigally in the one great effort he knew he had in him. It was his one chance[6]—now or not at all. His strength was waning[7] fast, and his hope was that before the last of it ebbed out of him[8] he would have beaten[9] his opponent down for the count. And as he continued to strike and force, coolly estimating the weight of his blows and the quality of the damage wrought[10], he realized how hard a man Sandel was to knock out. Stamina and

---

1 **upper cut:** golpe ascendente vertical • 2 **crumpled:** derrubou • 3 **had gone mad:** estava enlouquecida • 4 **it was to be:** seria • 5 **expended:** gastava • 6 **chance:** oportunidade • 7 **waning:** diminuía • 8 **ebbed out of him:** o abandonara • 9 **he would have beaten:** teria golpeado • 10 **the damage wrought:** o dano ocasionado

A PIECE OF STEAK 105

endurance were his to an extreme degree, and they were the virgin stamina and endurance of Youth. Sandel was certainly a coming man[1]. He had it in him. Only out of such rugged fibre were successful fighters fashioned[2].

Sandel was reeling[3] and staggering, but Tom King's legs were cramping and his knuckles going back on him[4]. Yet he steeled himself[5] to strike the fierce blows, every one of which brought anguish to his tortured hands. Though now he was receiving practically no punishment, he was weakening[6] as rapidly as the other. His blows went home, but there was no longer the weight behind them, and each blow was the result of a severe effort of will. His legs were like lead[7], and they dragged visibly under him[8]; while Sandel's backers, cheered by this symptom, began calling encouragement[9] to their man.

King was spurred to a burst of effort[10]. He delivered two blows in succession—a left, a trifle too high, to the solar plexus[11], and a right cross to the jaw. They were not heavy blows, yet so weak and dazed was Sandel that he went down and lay quivering[12]. The referee stood over him, shouting the count of the fatal seconds in his ear. If before the tenth second was called, he did not rise, the fight was lost. The house stood in hushed silence[13]. King rested on trembling

---

1 **a coming man:** uma promessa; homem com potencial, futuro • 2 **out of such rugged fibre were ... fashioned:** eram feitos dessa fibra resistente • 3 **was reeling:** vacilava • 4 **going back on him:** lhe falhavam • 5 **he steeled himself:** ele se encheu de força • 6 **he was weakening:** estava enfraquecendo • 7 **lead:** chumbo • 8 **they dragged visibly under him:** as arrastava visivelmente (as pernas) • 9 **calling encouragement:** animar • 10 **was spurred to a burst of effort:** ele se sentiu estimulado a fazer um esforço sobre-humano • 11 **solar plexus:** plexo solar • 12 **quivering:** tremendo • 13 **hushed silence:** silêncio sepulcral

legs. A mortal dizziness[1] was upon him, and before his eyes the sea of faces sagged and swayed[2], while to his ears, as from a remote distance, came the count of the referee. Yet he looked upon[3] the fight as his. It was impossible that a man so punished could rise.

Only Youth could rise, and Sandel rose. At the fourth second he rolled over on his face and groped[4] blindly for the ropes. By the seventh second he had dragged himself to his knee, where he rested, his head rolling groggily[5] on his shoulders. As the referee cried "Nine!" Sandel stood upright, in proper stalling position[6], his left arm wrapped about his face, his right wrapped about his stomach. Thus were his vital points guarded[7], while he lurched forward[8] toward King in the hope of effecting a clinch and gaining more time.

At the instant Sandel arose, King was at him, but the two blows he delivered were muffled[9] on the stalled arms. The next moment Sandel was in the clinch and holding on desperately while the referee strove[10] to drag the two men apart. King helped to force himself free. He knew the rapidity with which Youth recovered, and he knew that Sandel was his if he could prevent that recovery. One stiff[11] punch would do it[12]. Sandel was his, indubitably his. He had out-generalled him, out-fought him, out-pointed him[13]. Sandel

---

1 **dizziness:** vertigem • 2 **sagged and swayed:** se fundia e balançava • 3 **he looked upon:** considerava • 4 **groped:** tateava • 5 **groggily:** aturdido; grogue • 6 **in proper stalling question:** em clara posição de defesa • 7 **guarded:** protegidos • 8 **he lurched forward:** avançou cambaleando • 9 **were muffled:** ficaram amortecidos • 10 **strove:** se esforçava • 11 **stiff:** firme • 12 **would do it:** serviria • 13 **he had out-generalled him, out-fought him, out-pointed him:** o superara na estratégia, na luta e nos pontos

reeled out[1] of the clinch, balanced on the hair line between defeat or survival[2]. One good blow would topple him over and down and out[3]. And Tom King, in a flash of bitterness[4], remembered the piece of steak and wished that he had it then behind that necessary punch he must deliver. He nerved himself[5] for the blow, but it was not heavy enough nor swift enough. Sandel swayed, but did not fall, staggering back to the ropes and holding on. King staggered after him, and, with a pang[6] like that of dissolution, delivered another blow. But his body had deserted him[7]. All that was left of him was a fighting intelligence that was dimmed and clouded from exhaustion[8]. The blow that was aimed for the jaw struck no higher than the shoulder. He had willed[9] the blow higher, but the tired muscles had not been able to obey. And, from the impact of the blow, Tom King himself reeled back and nearly fell. Once again he strove. This time his punch missed altogether[10], and, from absolute weakness, he fell against Sandel and clinched, holding on to him[11] to save himself from[12] sinking to the floor.

King did not attempt to free himself. He had shot his bolt[13]. He was gone. And Youth had been served. Even in the clinch he could feel Sandel growing stronger against him.

---

1 **reeled out:** se livrou • 2 **balanced on the hair line between defeat or survival:** cambaleando na linha tênue que separa a derrota da sobrevivência • 3 **would topple him over and down and out:** ia desequilibrá-lo, derrubá-lo e nocauteá-lo • 4 **bitterness:** amargura • 5 **he nerved himself:** se encheu de coragem • 6 **pang:** pontada de dor • 7 **had deserted him:** o havia abandonado • 8 **dimmed and clouded from exhaustion:** enfraquecida e enevoada pela exaustão • 9 **he had willed:** havia desejado • 10 **his punch missed altogether:** errou o golpe totalmente • 11 **holding on to him:** agarrando-se a ele • 12 **to save himself from:** para evitar • 13 **he had shot his bolt:** tinha jogado a toalha

When the referee thrust them apart, there, before his eyes, he saw Youth recuperate. From instant to instant Sandel grew stronger. His punches, weak and futile at first, became stiff and accurate. Tom King's bleared[1] eyes saw the gloved fist driving at his jaw, and he willed to guard it by interposing his arm. He saw the danger, willed the act; but the arm was too heavy. It seemed burdened with a hundredweight of lead[2]. It would not lift itself, and he strove to lift it with his soul. Then the gloved fist landed home. He experienced a sharp snap[3] that was like an electric spark[4], and, simultaneously, the veil of blackness enveloped him[5].

When he opened his eyes again he was in his corner, and he heard the yelling of the audience like the roar of the surf[6] at Bondi Beach[7]. A wet sponge was being pressed against the base of his brain, and Sid Sullivan was blowing[8] cold water in a refreshing spray over his face and chest. His gloves had already been removed, and Sandel, bending over him[9], was shaking his hand. He bore no ill-will toward the man who had put him out[10] and he returned the grip[11] with a heartiness[12] that made his battered knuckles protest. Then Sandel stepped to the centre of the ring and the audience hushed[13] its pandemonium[14] to hear him accept young Pronto's challenge[15] and offer to increase the side bet to one hundred pounds.

---

1 **bleared:** ofuscados • 2 **it seemed burdened with a hundredweight of lead:** parecia sustentar uma tonelada de chumbo (*hundredweight* é uma unidade de massa equivalente a 45,36 kg) • 3 **sharp snap:** estalido agudo • 4 **spark:** faísca • 5 **enveloped him:** envolveu-o • 6 **surf:** surfe • 7 **Bondi Beach:** praia muito famosa de Sydney • 8 **was blowing:** estava jogando • 9 **bending over him:** inclinado sobre ele • 10 **had put him out:** o havia derrotado • 11 **he returned the grip:** devolveu o gesto • 12 **heartiness:** sinceridade • 13 **hushed:** acalmou • 14 **pandemonium:** pandemônio • 15 **challenge:** desafio

King looked on apathetically while his seconds mopped[1] the streaming water from him, dried his face, and prepared him to leave the ring. He felt hungry. It was not the ordinary, gnawing[2] kind, but a great faintness[3], a palpitation at the pit of the stomach[4] that communicated itself to all his body. He remembered back into the fight to the moment when he had Sandel swaying and tottering on the hair-line balance of defeat. Ah, that piece of steak would have done it! He had lacked just that for the decisive blow, and he had lost. It was all because of the piece of steak.

His seconds were half-supporting him[5] as they helped him through the ropes. He tore free from them, ducked through the ropes unaided[6], and leaped heavily to the floor, following on their heels[7] as they forced a passage for him down the crowded centre aisle. Leaving the dressing-room for the street, in the entrance to the hall, some young fellow spoke to him.

"W'y didn't yuh go in an' get 'im when yuh 'ad 'im?" the young fellow asked.

"Aw, go to hell!" said Tom King, and passed down the steps to the sidewalk[8].

The doors of the public-house[9] at the corner were swinging wide[10], and he saw the lights and the smiling barmaids[11], heard the many voices discussing the fight and the prosperous chink[12] of money on the bar. Somebody called to him

---

1 **mopped:** secavam • 2 **gnawing:** persistente • 3 **faintness:** fraqueza • 4 **pit of the stomach:** boca do estômago • 5 **were half-supporting him:** o sustentavam • 6 **unaided:** sem auxílio • 7 **following on their heels:** seguindo-os de perto • 8 **sidewalk:** calçada • 9 **public-house:** taverna; *pub* • 10 **swinging wide:** abertas de par em par • 11 **barmaids:** garçonetes • 12 **chink:** tinido

to have a drink. He hesitated perceptibly, then refused and went on his way.

He had not a copper[1] in his pocket, and the two-mile walk home seemed very long. He was certainly getting old. Crossing the Domain, he sat down suddenly on a bench, unnerved[2] by the thought of the missus sitting up for him[3], waiting to learn the outcome[4] of the fight. That was harder than any knockout, and it seemed almost impossible to face.

He felt weak and sore[5], and the pain of his smashed knuckles warned him[6] that, even if[7] he could find a job at navvy work, it would be a week before he could grip a pick handle[8] or a shovel[9]. The hunger palpitation at the pit of the stomach was sickening[10]. His wretchedness[11] overwhelmed him[12], and into his eyes came an unwonted moisture[13]. He covered his face with his hands, and, as he cried, he remembered Stowsher Bill and how he had served him[14] that night in the long ago. Poor old Stowsher Bill! He could understand now why Bill had cried in the dressing-room.

---

1 **copper:** moeda de cobre; centavo • 2 **unnerved:** nervoso • 3 **sitting up for him:** esperando-o acordada • 4 **outcome:** resultado • 5 **sore:** dolorido • 6 **warned him:** o alertavam • 7 **even if:** ainda que • 8 **pick handle:** picareta • 9 **shovel:** pá • 10 **sickening:** nauseante • 11 **wretchedness:** desgraça • 12 **overwhelmed him:** subjugou-o • 13 **unwonted moisture:** umidade inusitada • 14 **he had served him:** o havia derrotado